hmhco.com

The text was set in Adobe Garamond Pro.

Library of Congress Cataloging-in-Publication Data
Names: Hapka, Catherine.
Title: Clue by clue / Catherine Hapka.
Description: Boston ; New York : HMH Books for Young Readers, 2019. |
Series: Carmen Sandiego
Identifiers: LCCN 2018031761 | ISBN 9781328553089 (hardback)
Subjects: LCSH: Toy and movable books—Specimens. |
BISAC: JUVENILE FICTION / Media Tie-In. | JUVENILE FICTION
/ Interactive Adventures. | JUVENILE FICTION / Law & Crime.
Classification: LCC PZ7.H1996 Clu 2019 | DDC [Fic]—dc23
LC record available at https://lccn.loc.gov/2018031761

Manufactured in China
Leo 10 9 8 7 6 5 4 3 2 1
4500744987

CARMEN SANDIEGO™
CLUE BY CLUE

by Catherine Hapka

HOUGHTON MIFFLIN HARCOURT

BOSTON NEW YORK

LONDON

ST. PAUL'S
CATHEDRAL

TOWER OF
LONDON

BUCKINGHAM
PALACE

BIG BEN

TOWER BRIDGE

CHAPTER 1

London, England, 10:00 a.m., Local Time

CARMEN SANDIEGO PAUSED. HALF A BLOCK ahead, Tigress was strolling along the busy city street, stopping occasionally to glance into shop windows. With her razor-sharp claws tucked into the pockets of her stylish short trench coat, she looked like just another chic young Londoner. But Carmen knew better . . .

"Hey, Red, is our feline friend still window-shopping?" a voice spoke in Carmen's ear.

"That's what she wants everyone to think, Player," Carmen replied in a low voice. Her comm-link earrings could pick up even the quietest whisper—very handy, especially while tailing someone. "But I'm sure Tigress didn't come all this way to go on a five-fingered spree through London's blingiest boutiques."

Up ahead, Tigress stopped again and glanced around. Carmen ducked into a doorway. She held her breath. Had Tigress spotted her distinctive red fedora and trench coat? For a second, Carmen wondered if she should have gone incognito in a hoodie or something. Then again, it wouldn't have made much difference. Tigress wouldn't be fooled for a second—she knew Carmen's face as well as her own.

"All clear," Carmen murmured when Tigress moved on. Then Carmen hurried forward, not wanting to lose sight of her target. She'd been following Tigress through London, England, for half an hour. All the way from Victoria station to where they were now—the Knightsbridge neighborhood, according to Player. Very posh and exclusive. A shopper's mecca of high-end stores, from the world-famous Harrods department store to all sorts of designer boutiques—and some of the most expensive luxury apartments in the world.

Player loved finding out that kind of detail about the places Carmen visited. And he was good at it, too. No wonder—he was a high-tech whiz kid who spent most of his time exploring every bit and byte of the web. Carmen had never met Player in person, but he was a trusted part of her crew. Without his help, it would be a lot harder for her to carry out her self-appointed mission—traveling the world, righting wrongs, and stealing from criminals. In particular, the super-secret crime empire known as VILE.

Up ahead, Tigress suddenly dodged out of sight down an alley between a fancy restaurant—still closed at this early hour—and a large, stately old Victorian house. Carmen crept forward. Was this a trap? Tigress was clever—possibly the wiliest operative VILE had ever trained. Well, aside from Carmen herself, of course . . .

She caught up just in time to see Tigress slip into one of the buildings through a window. "She went into a house," she told Player.

"The one you're standing in front of right now? Hang on—I'll find out more." Player didn't leave her hanging for long. "Found it on GPS," he said. "That house belongs to a rich guy named Percival Weston-Blather. Fifty-four years old. No occupation listed."

"You had me at 'rich guy,'" Carmen said. "Mr. Weston-Blather must have something valuable in there."

"That would explain the chatter."

Carmen nodded, even though she knew Player couldn't see her. The "chatter," as he called it, was the reason she was here. Player was always nosing around the dark web, the regular web, and every cyber place in between for any secret signs or messages about VILE—Villains'

International League of Evil. The worst bunch of rogues and criminals that nobody ever heard of. Carmen's sworn nemesis. And her former family . . . well, sort of . . .

She shook those thoughts out of her head. "VILE is greedy," she whispered to Player. "But they wouldn't waste time and resources stealing some ordinary rich guy's gold watch and cuff links."

"Right. They've got to be after something big—something worth their effort," Player said.

Carmen nodded again. So what had they sent Tigress to steal this time?

"One way to find out," Carmen murmured, sidling closer to the open window and peeking in past the thick velvet floor-to-ceiling curtains. The curtains blocked most of the bright morning sunlight, but Carmen could see well enough once her eyes adjusted to the dimness within. "Whoa! Talk about a treasure trove!"

"What is it, Red?" Player whispered in her ear. "What kind of treasure are we talking about? Gold bars? High-tech equipment? Antique snuffboxes? What?"

Carmen's eyes swept the large room. It was set up like a museum exhibit, with glass-topped display cases instead of regular furniture. Framed documents and other stuff covered the walls.

"Pirate booty," she whispered. "Swords, axes, muskets, and a couple of full-size cannons. Chests full of gold doubloon coins and jewels. Even a big old tattered Jolly Roger!"

"The pirate flag," Player said.

Carmen nodded. "Looks like our rich guy is a collector."

Inside, Tigress had shed her trench coat, revealing the catsuit underneath. She'd swapped out her designer sunglasses for night-vision goggles that would make it easier to see in the dim room. Now she was moving toward one of the display cases at the far end. Carmen leaned forward, trying to see what the VILE operative was after.

"Doubloons, huh?" Player said. "Maybe VILE is trying to make up for those doubloons you stopped them from stealing in Ecuador recently. How much d'you think all that pirate booty is worth?"

"Plenty," Carmen replied softly. "But Tigress came on foot. How's she planning to get it all out of here?"

"Maybe VILE is sending some kind of transport."

"Maybe."

Carmen leaned forward as Tigress flexed the razor-sharp claws on the ends of her gloves and used one index finger to slice a hole in the glass case. Then the VILE operative pulled something out—a piece of ancient-looking parchment, yellowed, stained, and torn.

Tigress held it up to catch the light coming in through the windows, studying it. Carmen's eyes widened as she, too, got a better look. It appeared to be a map. Could it be a treasure map?

She pulled a compact mirror out of her pocket. Only it wasn't really a compact — it was a high-tech optical scanner. Even from this distance, she should be able to get a pretty good image of that map . . .

Click!

Tigress whirled around at the almost inaudible sound of the scanner. "You!" she cried.

CHAPTER 2

CARMEN BARELY HAD TIME TO SHOVE THE compact in her pocket before Tigress was on her, a whirling dervish of claws and hair and angry shrieks. She yanked Carmen in through the window, diving at her face with those claws.

"Well, well—look what the cat dragged in!" she cried, her eyes flashing with fury.

Carmen pulled free, ducking and rolling out of reach. But just barely . . .

"What's the map for, Tigress?" she asked, diving toward the scrap of paper, which Tigress had dropped.

"Not so fast," Tigress snarled, snatching it up and

shoving it into her sleeve. "That belongs to me. But you can have *this* if you want it!"

She grabbed a cannonball and hurled it at Carmen, who ducked aside just in time. *CRASH!* A display case full of telescopes, astrolabes, and other old navigation tools exploded, sending glass flying like shrapnel. Carmen leaped away, grabbing a pirate cutlass sword from a display rack as she tucked and rolled past.

"No thanks," she said, swinging the cutlass. "I prefer this."

Tigress grabbed a long saber and blocked the swing. "Nice try," she growled, attacking with a swing of her own.

CLANG! The swords met again and again, two fighters equally matched. Carmen almost smiled, flashing back to her days at VILE Academy, when she and Tigress had sparred this way countless times in Coach Brunt's Combat & Weaponry class. Back when this sort of thing had seemed like innocent fun . . .

"Hey!" she blurted out as Tigress struck again — this time flinging Carmen's blade right out of her hand!

Uh-oh. She couldn't get distracted — not while she was dealing with Tigress. Carmen somersaulted away, kicking out as she passed and hitting her foe square in the elbow.

"Ow!" Tigress shrieked, dropping her saber, which Carmen knocked away as she rolled past.

When she looked up, Tigress was already coming at her again, this time with a pike, a long wooden pole with a blade on the end. Carmen grabbed a small round shield —from Coach Brunt's class, she knew it was called a buckler, as in swashbuckler—and used it to fend off the blows. The whole time, she kept part of her attention on the bit of parchment sticking out of Tigress's sleeve. One of the things she'd learned from VILE was how to pick a pocket without the mark even noticing.

Of course, that was the one final exam I never managed to pass, she reminded herself, her mind flashing briefly to the disapproving look on Shadowsan's face that day . . .

"Yikes!" she exclaimed, barely dodging another jab of the pike.

"Red? You okay?" Player cried in her ear.

"Fine, fine," she muttered. "Having the time of my life."

"Talking to yourself, Black Sheep?" Tigress spat out Carmen's former code name from crime school as if it tasted bad. "That's a sign that you're losing it, you know. Let me do you a favor and put you out of your misery!"

She swung the pike again. Carmen ducked and leaped forward, reaching for the edge of the parchment as Tigress whirled past.

"Now, now, now!" Tigress shrank back from Carmen's fingers just in time. "I told you, that's mine!"

"Only as long as you can keep it." Carmen grabbed a wooden ship's wheel and used it to hook Tigress's pike, flinging it out of her hand. All Carmen needed was one good chance . . .

She dove forward, grabbing for the parchment again. This time Tigress leaped up, somersaulting over Carmen's head and landing behind her. Carmen spun around, then paused to catch her breath and study the opposition. Tigress backed away, watching Carmen warily.

Carmen realized she had the enemy just where she wanted her — backed into a corner of the room with no doors or windows. She gathered herself to attack again . . .

"Oh, look!" Tigress's voice suddenly went sugar-sweet. "A little doggy came to check out the kitty cat."

Carmen looked over and saw the dog — a cute, furry little thing with floppy ears. It had just wandered in from another room, wagging its tail as if asking to join the game.

"Sorry, puppy," Tigress sang out. "Don't you know cats and dogs don't get along?"

"No!" Carmen cried as Tigress grabbed an axe, flinging it at the dog.

Acting on instinct, Carmen grabbed a worn leather pirate hat and leaped forward, doing a dive roll. She shoved the hat out like a catcher's mitt, and the axe embedded itself in the three-sided brim.

"Oof!" she grunted as she hit the floor with a thud. Out of the corner of her eye, she saw Tigress leaping out through the window.

The dog barked happily, rushing over to lick Carmen's cheek as she lay there for a second breathing hard.

"Red?" Player sounded worried.

"I'm okay," she replied wearily, reaching over to scratch the dog behind the ears. "But Tigress got away—with that parchment."

"No biggie," Player told her. "I got the scan. And I think I know what VILE is after . . ."

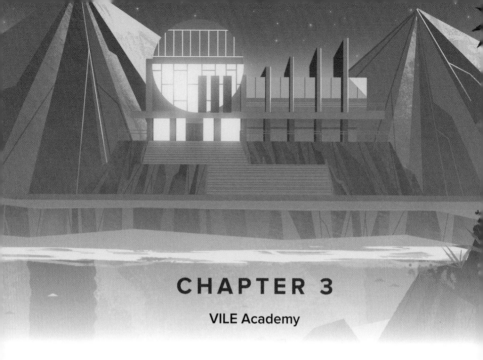

CHAPTER 3

VILE Academy

Professor Maelstrom strode into the gothic-meets-ultramodern room at the heart of VILE Academy known simply as the faculty lounge. The others were already there waiting. Dr. Saira Bellum was staring intently at the lines of numbers and scientific formulas on a glowing green hologram screen hanging before her in midair. Countess Cleo lounged in her high-backed chair, looking bored as she played with the sparkling diamond bracelet hanging from one slender wrist. Coach Brunt drummed her thick fingers impatiently on the table. And Shadowsan, as always, sat so still he could have been carved from stone.

"Well?" Countess Cleo spoke first. "Any word from the queen of the jungle?"

"Indeed." A slow smile spread over Maelstrom's gaunt face. "Tigress has the map in hand." His smile faded slightly. "Though she did encounter a slight . . . er . . . delay."

"What kind of delay?" As always, Coach Brunt's words were short, to the point, and delivered with a slight Texas twang.

"A certain . . . Red Menace." Maelstrom grimaced.

"Black Sheep," Shadowsan pronounced. It was a statement, not a question.

Dr. Bellum looked up from her screen and frowned. "How did she find out about the treasure?"

"Never mind that," Maelstrom said. "The important thing is that Tigress escaped with the map. And of course, we have something that Carmen Sandiego has no idea about . . ."

He cackled, fingering a round item before tucking it away again. Dr. Bellum and Countess Cleo smiled, and Coach Brunt barked out a laugh. Only Shadowsan remained grim.

"You thought she had no idea about the map," he reminded Maelstrom. "And yet she did."

"Good point." Dr. Bellum nodded. "Has Tigress

passed off the map to another operative yet? Safer that way, especially with Carmen Sandiego lurking around. Protocol, you know."

"I know." Maelstrom didn't bother to remind her that he'd invented the protocol. "And no, she hasn't passed it on yet. For this particular situation, I have something different in mind . . ."

CHAPTER 4

London, England, Several Hours Later

AND YOU DID NOT SEE ANYONE ENTER OR LEAVE ze premises?" Inspector Chase Devineaux demanded for the third time, his French accent extra-thick with frustration.

Several hours earlier he'd sneaked into his old Interpol office to retrieve his belongings. All the while, he was stewing over whether to join the mysterious crime-fighting organization known only as ACME. On the one hand, he supposed it was an honor to be asked. On the other hand, they had invited Julia Argent as well. She was his partner at Interpol, though he still wasn't sure why he'd gotten stuck with her — she was merely a rookie, and talked far too much. If ACME valued someone like her as much as a master investigator like him, was it worth leaving Interpol to join them? It was almost an insult, really! That was why he'd stormed out after receiving the invitation, telling the mysterious Chief that he'd have to think over her offer.

Besides that, ACME had arranged the transfer from his old job before even asking him. The nerve! That alone was almost enough to make Devineaux say no. Almost. Because the truth was, he'd had little luck capturing the world's most famous thief, Carmen Sandiego, during his time as an Interpol agent. Perhaps ACME would be able to provide him with better resources . . .

Before he could reach a decision, he'd heard a ping from his cellphone. It was a text from one of his contacts in London — one who hadn't yet heard that Devineaux was no longer with Interpol, though he didn't bother to update him at that moment. Because the contact was reporting a rumor that Carmen Sandiego had just struck at a collector's home in Knightsbridge! Devineaux had dropped everything immediately and caught the first train out of France. The notorious Carmen Sandiego was the one criminal who had managed to elude him many times over. By now she was his obsession, his white whale. How lucky to receive this tip now, just when he thought she'd escaped his grasp. He was determined to bring her to justice, no matter what it took.

But once he'd reached the scene of the crime,

Devineaux hadn't been able to find out much more. The homeowner, a certain Monsieur Weston-Blather, seemed to know nothing about what had happened.

"I told you, I was out at the time—I take my morning constitutional every day at precisely ten a.m., rain or shine," Weston-Blather said, puffing out his ample belly and frowning at Devineaux over the tops of his spectacles. He waved a hand at the mess surrounding them. "Imagine my consternation, arriving home to find this! My beloved collection—plundered!"

Devineaux glanced around. Collection? It looked more like a jumble of old junk to him. "And yet nothing of value was taken?" he said.

"What?!" Weston-Blather puffed up even more, his bulbous nose going red with outrage. "I already told you, sir: a valuable old parchment is missing!"

"A parchment, eh?" Devineaux was starting to wonder if this was a wild goose chase. Still, if there was even a chance that Carmen Sandiego had been here . . .

His phone vibrated in his pocket. He pulled it out, grimacing when he saw that it was Julia Argent calling. It really rankled that she'd horned in on his job offer . . .

"I expect you to retrieve my property posthaste, sir!" Weston-Blather's loud voice interrupted Devineaux's thoughts. "Have you any leads?"

"Er, of course." Devineaux glanced around again.

"Why do you suppose she didn't take the jewels, or the gold coins? Are you sure none of those are missing?"

"She?" The man peered at him sharply. "She who? Do you have a suspect?"

Devineaux knew better than to share leads with a civilian. Best to change the subject, give himself a chance to think . . . "This . . . ah . . . parchment you say has gone missing," he said. "It's valuable, then?"

"Quite!" Weston-Blather said proudly. "The *Times* recently ran a feature story about my collection of pirate paraphernalia—featuring that very parchment! Although . . ." He leaned forward, glancing from side to side as if ascertaining that nobody would overhear. Since the only other soul in sight was a small, scruffy dog sniffing around the base of a heavy velvet curtain, he seemed satisfied that he could continue: ". . . there was one detail I kept secret. You see, that parchment is the only known copy of a map—to a treasure that has never been found!"

Devineaux frowned, once again wondering if he was wasting his valuable time. Treasure maps? Pirates? What foolishness!

"Very well," he said. "Perhaps that is all I need to—"

"But it's not just any treasure map!" Weston-Blather interrupted. "It was hand drawn by the seventeenth-century pirate Cal Cutlass! He sailed with the notorious Captain Goldtooth's crew, and one day he stole the entire ship's bounty and spirited it away. Not so much as a single doubloon of that treasure was ever seen again!"

"That may be," Devineaux broke in. "Now really, sir, I must —"

But once again, Weston-Blather cut him off. "Naturally, I've been studying the map ever since I acquired it," he said. "But it shows only a small area of beach and sea, with no hint as to its location." He shrugged. "Well, unless it's in code — there are some crude symbols drawn at the top of the page . . ."

"Ridiculous!" Devineaux burst out, unable to contain his impatience any longer. "Why would Car — er — why would anyone bother to steal such a thing?"

Weston-Blather was staring into space, not seeming to hear Devineaux's comment. "And what a bother that this should happen only a day before Cal Cutlass's diary goes on display right here in London!" He clasped his meaty fists. "If only I'd gotten a look at that diary first, perhaps it might have offered some hint . . ."

"Eh?" Devineaux perked up. Now, *this* could be a clue! "Diary, you say? What diary? What display? Where?"

"The British Museum recently acquired a diary said

to have been written by Cal Cutlass himself," Weston-Blather explained. "It's to be unveiled as part of a special exhibit at the Tower of London. For you see, many pirates were imprisoned in the area while awaiting their turns at nearby Execution Dock, and so —"

"The Tower of London?" This time Devineaux was the one to interrupt. "And this diary is there now, you say?"

"Why, yes, it should be. As I mentioned, the exhibit opens tomorrow."

For the first time since his arrival, Devineaux smiled. "Then that is where Carmen Sandiego shall strike next!" he cried, striding toward the exit so fast that he nearly tripped over the little dog, which was still nosing around the curtains. "I'm afraid I must go, monsieur. Good day!"

Weston-Blather watched him depart. "Interpol certainly is hiring some odd ducks these days," he commented. Then he shrugged and hurried out of the room himself.

As the man's footsteps faded, a figure stepped out from behind the curtains. Carmen's eyes twinkled as she glanced out the window after Inspector Devineaux, who was already nearly out of sight and moving fast.

"I'm impressed," she murmured to the little dog,

bending to feed it another treat. "Inspector Chase Devineaux is getting to know me pretty well!"

The dog barked and wagged its tail. Carmen gave it one last pat, then straightened up.

"Player, you there?" she said. "Let's get this show on the road."

CHAPTER 5

On the Road to the Tower of London, Midnight

T HE OLD-FASHIONED BLACK LONDON TAXI PEELED around the corner onto another nearly deserted city street. "Take it easy, Zack!" Carmen exclaimed. "I want to get there in one piece."

Zack grinned at her, his eyes twinkling in his freckled face. "Hey, I'm s'posed to be a cabbie, right?" he said in his thick Boston accent.

"You're a *London* cabbie, bro," his sister Ivy informed him from the back seat. "They're, like, way more genteel than the ones back home."

Carmen smiled. The two former Boston street kids might seem loud and goofy and even a little crazy to some people, but she knew she could count on them for anything. They were just as important to her team as Player in their own ways.

Speaking of Player . . . "Find anything else on our pirate?" she asked through her earpiece.

"Pirate?" Zack glanced over so fast the car veered halfway into the next lane. "What about pirates?"

"That's whose diary we're after," Carmen told him and Ivy. "A pirate named Cal Cutlass who sailed with Captain Goldtooth."

"Cool—I love pirates!" Zack exclaimed. "Tell me more!"

Carmen nodded. As Player told her what he'd learned, she repeated it for Zack and Ivy. "Apparently Cal Cutlass was one of the most notorious members of one of the most dastardly crews in pirate history. It's rumored that he plucked out his own eye to scare his victims, and that was why Cal always wore an eye patch." She grabbed the armrest as the taxi peeled around another corner. "Captain Goldtooth's crew cut a swath of looting and destruction throughout the Caribbean and beyond."

"That's right," Player said in her ear. "They amassed a huge amount of treasure—which suddenly went missing. Cal Cutlass was fingered for the dirty deed and betrayed in turn by his crewmates by being turned over to the authorities. He was dragged off to stand trial right there in London, but ended up escaping. Neither he nor the treasure was ever seen again."

"Wow," Carmen said. Then she told the others what Player had said.

"Really?" Ivy looked interested. "So that map you snapped the pic of . . ."

"Might be Cal Cutlass's treasure map," Carmen finished for her. "But the trick is, where in the world is the beach on the map?"

She grabbed her phone and scrolled over to the enhanced image of the parchment Player had sent her earlier. The map showed ocean, beach, trees, rock formations . . . but nothing else. No X-marks-the-spot where the treasure might be buried. And nothing specifying anything else about the location. Just a line of mysterious little pictures and symbols at the top of the page. A code? If so, neither she nor Player had any idea what it might mean.

She lowered the phone and stared out the window at the twinkling lights of London, thinking hard. "VILE wanted that map badly enough to send one of their best operatives to get it," she mused aloud. "Which means they think they can use it to find Cal Cutlass's treasure."

"Yeah," Player agreed. "Maybe this diary can help us beat them to it."

"Hope so. Unless Tigress gets her greedy paws on the diary first." Carmen grimaced at the thought.

"I'm not sure VILE even knows about the diary, Red," Player replied. "I hacked into security footage at Heathrow, and Tigress left on a charter flight a couple of hours ago."

"Interesting," Carmen said. "Maybe they know something we don't know. Like where that beach is located." She glanced forward. There wasn't much traffic at this late hour, and they were making good time. A stone fortress was already rising into view up ahead. "But we'll have to worry about that later. I think I see the target."

"The Tower of London, you mean?" Player said. "Pretty cool, right? It was built by William the Conqueror around 1078 or so. Over the years since then it's been a lookout, a palace, a treasure vault, a prison—even a private zoo!"

"You know I love your history lessons, Player," Carmen broke in with a smile. "But we'll have to pick it up after

I grab that diary, okay? Because we're here." The cab screeched to a halt beside a tall stone wall. "Okay, wish me luck," Carmen told her crew, stepping out of the car. "Meet you around the corner in a few minutes."

"We'll be waiting." Zack gunned the engine of the cab and took off.

The streets around the Tower were deserted at this hour. But Carmen pulled her red fedora down to hide her face, just in case Player was wrong and VILE was watching. Then she headed for the high stone wall, already reaching for the grappling hook tucked into the lining of her trench coat.

"Security cameras disabled, right?" she murmured.

"Right," Player responded in her ear. "But you'll have to hurry. I put the footage on a loop, but someone'll probably notice at some point."

Carmen didn't bother to respond. She sent the grappler flying into the dark, listening until it hooked into place with a soft *clink*.

Seconds later, she was landing on the ground inside the tall stone walls. "Wow, this place is cool," she commented, glancing around. The moonlight offered a pretty good view of the ancient fortress grounds, which consisted of various inner towers, walls, and buildings, along with grassy areas and pathways. It was like stepping back in time! Well, except for the electric safety lights and the signs pointing the way to the gift shop, of course.

"The pirate exhibit is in Wakefield Tower," Player told her. "It's over near the river—you can cut across to get there. You're looking for the round building next to Bloody Tower."

Carmen followed his directions, moving quickly past some ancient buildings into a central green. To her right stood the White Tower, one of the oldest parts of the ancient fortress, located at the center of the complex, but Carmen barely spared it a glance as she hurried on. "Hey, check out the birds," she said as she spotted several large, shiny black birds snoozing inside a modern enclosure nearby. "Those must be the famous Tower ravens, huh?"

"Yup," Player said. "There's a legend that if the ravens ever leave, the Tower—and the entire kingdom—will fall. But never mind that. You're almost there."

"Copy that." Carmen followed a sign pointing the way to the special pirate exhibition. Once inside, she scanned the room and soon spotted an ancient book with a leather cover. It was enclosed in a clear display case. "Okay, I've located the target," she told Player. "Preparing to acquire it."

"Roger that," Player said. "Cameras and alarms still offline."

Carmen whipped a small item out of her trench coat. It looked like an ordinary tube of mascara, but it was actually a glass cutter. One quick slice, and the case was open — and the diary was in her pocket.

"Got it," she hissed, backing quickly away.

"Good. Now get out of there!" Player urged.

She took his advice, sprinting out of the exhibit. Up ahead, one of the ravens let out a sudden, rusty caw. Carmen skidded to a stop, listening. What had awakened the bird? Was someone there?

"Think I'll take a shortcut, Player," she whispered, turning and racing toward the closest exterior wall, located beside the famous Traitors' Gate that led out to the Thames. "I'm not sure I'm alone. Inspector Devineaux could have tipped off the guards that I might be here tonight."

"Doesn't seem like his style. He wants to take you down himself, right?"

"Better safe than sorry. I'm out of here."

She wasted no time sending her grappling hook flying. Soon she was landing softly on the lawn outside the main wall. The River Thames lay just a few yards ahead. Carmen took a step toward it, admiring the way the moonlight sparkled on the current. Sometimes she got so busy trying to take down VILE that she forgot to stop and admire the scenery . . .

"*Excusez-moi!*" a voice rang out immediately behind her. "Stop right there, Carmen Sandiego!"

Carmen gulped. She knew that voice . . .

She spun around, cursing herself for losing focus, as Chase Devineaux stepped out of the darkness. She'd known he was likely to be lurking about—why hadn't she kept a better lookout for him?

"What are you doing here?" she exclaimed, pretending to be surprised to see him.

He smirked. "Wouldn't you like to know my secrets?" he said. "No, the only important thing for you to know is that you are under arrest, by the authority of Interpol!"

Carmen raised an eyebrow, carefully keeping just out of arm's reach. "What are the charges, monsieur?"

"What are the . . ." Devineaux sputtered for a few seconds, stalking toward her as she backed toward the river. "Are you kidding me, Carmen Sandiego? I just caught you breaking into the Tower of London! What did you steal—the Crown Jewels? Perhaps St Edward's Crown?"

Carmen patted her pockets. "Nope, no crown in here."

Devineaux rolled his eyes. "You think you are so clever, eh? Well, tell me—how clever is it to commit your dastardly crimes while wearing that silly bright red hat and coat?"

"Hmm, you may have a point." Carmen shrugged. "Then again, I wouldn't want to be without my tools."

She reached into one of the coat's interior pockets. "Like this, for instance . . ."

She pulled out a small canister of super-slick grease. Devineaux squinted at it.

"Is that a weapon?" he demanded.

"Not exactly." Carmen bent and sprayed the sidewalk between herself and the inspector. "It won't hurt you — as long as you stay where you are until it dries."

"What?" Devineaux sounded outraged. "You cannot tell me what to do, Carmen Sandiego!" He took a step forward. *"Mon Dieu!"* he cried in alarm as he immediately slipped halfway across the riverside walkway.

Carmen took a step backwards. "No, seriously," she said. "You might want to stand still. Otherwise . . ."

"Are you not listening to my words?" he exclaimed. "If you are not careful, I will have you on resisting arrest as well, Carmen Sand — argh!"

He took another step, which sent him flying across the rest of the walkway. He hit the waist-high railing separating land from river, arms flailing as he scrabbled at the railing, fighting to catch his balance.

"Careful!" Carmen called. "Just grab the — oops, too late."

She winced as Devineaux tipped forward over the railing, feet flying, then disappeared from view . . .

SPLASH!

"What was that, Red?" Player hissed in her ear. "Is everything going okay?"

"Swimmingly, Player." She stepped forward and glanced down. Devineaux was sputtering with fury while treading water in the murky, chilly Thames. Oh well—he couldn't say she hadn't warned him . . . "Where are Zack and Ivy?"

"Corner of Water Lane and Lower Thames Street," Player replied. "Want me to send them to pick you up?"

"No, that's okay—I'll find them. Tell Zack to start the engine."

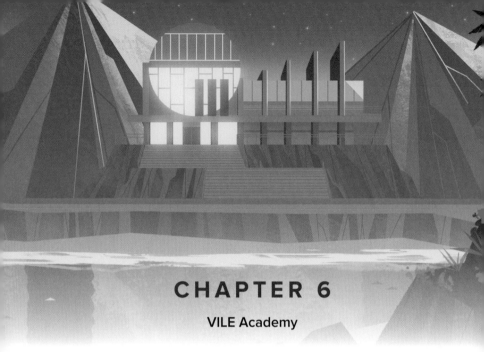

CHAPTER 6

VILE Academy

T IGRESS STALKED INTO THE FACULTY LOUNGE. "Why did you make me come back here?" she demanded, glaring at Professor Maelstrom and the other four teachers seated in their high-backed chairs. "I already have the map. I'm ready to find that treasure!"

"Easy, kitten," Maelstrom said with a smirk. Tigress could be impertinent—nearly as much so as another former student—but he couldn't help but admire her spirit. "All things in time, mmm?"

"Yeah, Professor Maelstrom thought you might need a little backup on this one," Coach Brunt put in. Then she let out a sharp whistle.

Hearing footsteps behind her, Tigress spun around.

There in the doorway stood several of her fellow operatives—Le Chèvre, El Topo, and Mime Bomb.

"What are *they* doing here?" she demanded, spinning around again to face Maelstrom.

"As Coach Brunt mentioned, I've decided it would be best to make this one a group effort," Maelstrom said. "Consider these three to be your loyal pirate crew for the duration of the operation."

"*What?!?*" Tigress's shriek was so loud that Dr. Bellum's glowing green virtual screen flickered. "I *don't* need help—I work alone!"

"My decision is final." Maelstrom's voice was calm but held an edge of steel that even Tigress couldn't ignore. "With Carmen Sandiego hot on your trail, there is no time to lose. Besides, this is a treasure hunt—that means you're likely to need someone who can dig."

Tigress shrugged, realizing he was right. El Topo's name was Spanish for "The Mole" because his specialty was digging. As in, digging for treasure. Why wear herself out when he could do the dirty work?

El Topo stepped forward with a flourish and squared his broad shoulders. "It will be my pleasure to work with you again, my feline friend."

"And I shall act as your lookout," Le Chèvre proclaimed. "The treasure map shows several large rock outcroppings, and who better to climb them for a better view, *oui?*" Le Chèvre, also known as "The Goat," was all about climbing buildings and mountains and any other kind of high places.

"Okay, I guess that's true," Tigress said grudgingly. She glared at Mime Bomb. "But what about *him?*"

Mime Bomb grinned and sashayed forward, waving his arms around in a way that seemed to mean something, though Tigress didn't have the fuzziest idea what he was trying to say—as usual.

Coach Brunt chuckled. "Mime Bomb, figuring out what you're tryin' to tell us is about as easy as puttin' socks on a rooster," she said. "Heck of a code breaker, though."

Mime Bomb swept into an elaborate bow toward both professors, then snapped to attention and saluted Tigress.

"Yes, Mime Bomb has a real talent for symbology and cryptanalysis," Maelstrom said. "And as you may have noticed, Tigress, there is a line of code at the top of the map."

"You mean those weird little drawings of boats and anchors and stuff?" She pulled out the map and waved it at Mime Bomb. "Okay, Code Boy, so what does it mean? I spent the whole flight here trying to figure it out, and nothing!"

"That's because you were missing a vital element, my dear." Countess Cleo nodded toward Mime Bomb. "Show her the treasure you found on your previous heist—the one that will lead us to this treasure." She clinked her jeweled bracelets for emphasis.

Mime Bomb reached into one pocket, then another, turning them inside out and coming up empty. Tigress crossed her arms and watched him, tapping one foot impatiently.

"Seriously?" she growled. "This is a waste of time!"

"So is trying to decipher a treasure code without the decoder," Shadowsan said in his usual gruff voice.

"Decoder?" Tigress echoed.

Mime Bomb grinned and raised one finger in an "aha!" gesture. He lifted his hat, then reached up and plucked something off his head—a small, round metal object, worn with age.

"The decoder," Maelstrom said. "Mime Bomb discovered this on a recent heist and knew it must be the key to something grand. He will be in charge of using it to decipher the symbols on the map, which should lead you to that legendary treasure."

"Indeed," Cleo said, rubbing her hands together so hard that her rings clinked.

"Indubitably." Dr. Bellum looked up from her screen and grinned.

"Sure as shootin'!" Coach Brunt added with a whoop.

Tigress let out a soft growl. She was still annoyed at being stuck with a bunch of other operatives for this important mission. But it was clear that the entire faculty agreed with Maelstrom's stupid pirate crew plan—which meant there wasn't much point in arguing.

"Fine, whatever." She glared at the other operatives. "But *I'm* in charge of the mission, okay? Now, come on— Carmen Sandiego is out there somewhere, you know. So let's stop wasting time here." She tossed the map at Mime Bomb. "You can decode this on the way."

T*HAT'S WHAT THIS WHOLE HEIST WAS FOR?*" Ivy said in disbelief. "Some dusty old *book?*"

Carmen was back in the cab, where she'd just shown Zack and Ivy her prize. "Uh-huh," she told them. "Now let's see if it has any clues for us."

She flipped open the soft, well-worn leather cover. Inside were words written in a faded, old-fashioned hand-writing:

Diary of Cal Cutlass, Pirate

"What's it say?" Zack asked from behind the wheel. Horns honked as he cut across several lanes of traffic.

"Oops," he added. "I keep forgetting they drive on the wrong side of the road over here."

"So what?" Ivy said with a laugh. "You drive on *both* sides of the road back home, and it never bothered you before!"

Carmen ignored them, carefully flipping the delicate pages. "Okay, looks like this is just what it sounds like," she said, scanning the words written there. "Cal Cutlass just joined the crew of a notorious pirate named Captain Goldtooth—"

"Cool name, right?" Zack put in, spinning the wheel to avoid a double-decker bus. "I always thought my pirate name should be Zackbeard. Get it? Zackbeard the pirate?"

Ivy rolled her eyes. "More like Zackweird!"

"Hang on, we're there." Zack turned the car down an alley.

"We're where?" Ivy asked, glancing around at several storefronts with signs in Chinese.

Zack grinned. "Dinner!" he said. "Namely, the best noodles in London. I called ahead."

Carmen's stomach rumbled, and she realized none of them had eaten for hours. "Okay, but get it to go," she said. "I want to read more of this diary, and we can't do that where anyone might see. VILE has eyes everywhere."

A few minutes later, the three of them were perched on a rooftop overlooking Trafalgar Square. The streets of London were nearly deserted as the hour grew later, and a light breeze ruffled the diary pages as Carmen flipped through them between bites of stir-fry.

Zack licked hot-and-sour sauce off his fingers. "So what's this pirate guy have to say, Carm?" he asked.

"Not a whole lot so far." Carmen went on. "Cal is pretty excited at being allowed to join even though he's only fifteen. Basically, he's psyched to be a pirate, and this diary is where he'll record all his adventures on the high seas . . ."

Ivy dumped the rest of the noodles onto her plate, then peered at the diary over Carmen's shoulder. "Great. I'll wait for the movie," she commented.

Carmen chuckled. "Not sure this one will make it into theaters," she said, flipping another page. "The first few pages look like they're mostly just bragging about how tough Cal is and how cool it is to be a pirate." She flipped a few more pages. "I hope there's something more—hey, look!"

Several of the wrinkled old pages had stuck together, causing the diary to fall open to the very last page. Scribbled there were two long columns—one the letters of the alphabet, and the other a series of symbols like jewels, skulls, and scimitars. Both columns were faded and a little smudged, but a few of the symbols looked familiar . . .

"Check it out!" Ivy was peering over Carmen's shoulder again, pointing with her chopsticks. "Is that, like, a code or something?"

"Looks like it." Carmen pulled out her compact and scanned the page. "Hey, Player, I'm sending you something—do these symbols match up with the ones on the parchment Tigress stole?"

"Wait, what's that sketch in the corner?" Ivy was still leaning over Carmen's shoulder. "Looks like plans for some kinda gadget!"

"A decoder!" Carmen said. "Did that part come

through on the scan, Player?" She tapped a button on her phone so all three of them could hear his response.

"Yep, I see it," Player said. "And I think you're right, Red. The symbols on the list are the same as the ones on the map. It looks like a basic one-for-one replacement code—each symbol represents a letter of the alphabet. Anyone with that decoder could just spin the wheel to match them up."

"I wonder if Cal Cutlass made a decoder based on this drawing," Carmen said, thinking aloud. "If so, I bet VILE got their mitts on it somehow, which explains why they decided to steal the map—and why they didn't need this diary."

"Yeah." Zack's eyes widened. "Tigress could already be on the way to finding that pirate booty! Shiver me timbers!"

Ivy snorted. "Lame, bro."

"Arrrrr. Talking like a pirate is fun, matey." Zack flicked a grain of rice in her direction.

Meanwhile Carmen was staring at the symbols in the diary, drawn hundreds of years ago by a ruthless young pirate. Could they really be the key to a vast treasure? If so, she was going to do her best to make sure the equally ruthless VILE didn't get their greedy paws on it . . .

"Hey, let me get a look at those plans," Ivy said. She

was all about gadgets and was always tinkering with something. Carmen handed the diary over.

"Think you can make one?" she asked.

"Sure, just give me a sec . . ." Ivy pulled a utility knife out of her pocket, then grabbed one of the empty Chinese takeout containers.

A few minutes later, Ivy held up a double circle of cardboard with a joint in the middle formed out of the wire handle from the takeout box.

Carmen smiled. "Hey, Player," she said. "You should see this decoder that Ivy just built."

"Whoa." Zack looked up from his food, eyes wide. "You built that just now, sis? Out of Chinese takeout cartons?"

"Dude, I can build anything," Ivy said. "Anytime, anywhere, out of *any* kind of takeout carton."

"How's it look?" Player asked.

"Looks like a little round doodad full of letters and pictures." Zack sounded dubious. "How does it work?"

"Like this." Ivy held up the decoder. "You pick a symbol from our map, okay? How's about . . ." She leaned over to see the scanned image of the treasure map on Carmen's phone. "Okay, take this little skull and crossbones," she went on. "You spin the dial until it shows up in this here little window on the top . . ."

She demonstrated. Carmen leaned closer. "And then

you look at the letter that shows up in the opening on the other side," Carmen said. "In this case, R."

"Very high-tech," Player said dryly.

"It's old-school-tech, dude," Ivy said with a grin. "Wicked cool, right?"

"For sure," Carmen agreed. "Let's give it a whirl."

She zoomed in on the map and examined the line of symbols:

"Okay, first symbol is a curved knife—a scimitar, maybe?" Carmen said.

"Let me try." Zack grabbed the decoder out of his sister's hand and twirled the dial. "Curved sword thingy? That's a letter S."

"Next comes an anchor . . ." One by one, Carmen read out the symbols. As the siblings called out the corresponding letters, she wrote them down.

When they finished, Carmen picked up the paper and studied the message:

SEEK MORGAN'S STONE IN LOST HAVEN WITH WATER ALL AROUND

"What the heck does that mean?" Ivy wondered, picking at the last few noodles on her plate.

"I'm not sure yet," Carmen said.

"Aw, man—another puzzle?" Zack complained. "Where's the decoder to help us figure this one out?"

Carmen was already keyboarding the message into her laptop. "What do you think, Player?" she said.

"Already researching pirate history for ideas," Player replied. "Morgan probably refers to Sir Henry Morgan, the famous privateer—that's basically another name for pirate."

"Maybe Captain Goldtooth stole some jewels from this Morgan guy," Ivy guessed. "Jewels . . . stones—get it? It could just be telling us we're after the treasure."

"What about the lost haven?" Zack said, sitting up and looking interested. "I've heard there were pirate havens all around the Caribbean back then, where honest men would never dare to set foot for fear of being robbed and stuff." At his sister's surprised look, he shrugged. "What? I saw a pirate special on TV once."

"First hit on pirate havens is Tortuga, a small island off the coast of Haiti," Player said.

"An island? That's gotta be it!" Zack said. "Water all around—get it?"

"Cool—let's go to Tortuga!" Ivy exclaimed. "Book us a flight, Player!"

"Wait." Carmen frowned, staring thoughtfully out over the city. "What about the 'lost' part? That's got to mean something, right? And I have a feeling the 'water all around' part means something more specific than just an island, too . . . Keep looking."

"Yeah—water all around?" Ivy rolled her eyes at her brother. "Duh—that's *every* island, bro! Nantucket, Aruba, Manhattan, Australia . . ."

"Whatever, sis." Zack shrugged. "I never said I was a puzzle expert, okay?"

"Hang on—I think I found it," Player announced. "You're right, Red—there *is* a lost pirate haven out there! It's Port Royal, Jamaica—a former pirate town ruled by none other than Henry Morgan. It sank into the sea after an earthquake in 1692!"

"So this Port Royal place is underwater?" Ivy exclaimed. "Water all around, right?"

"Right. Guess I'd better bring my diving gear." Carmen smiled, though she couldn't help feeling a little uneasy. They were on their way, but Tigress had a pretty good head start. And if she had the original decoder, it probably hadn't taken her long to work out the clue—not with the evil masterminds of VILE helping her. Were Carmen and her crew already too late? Only one way to find out . . . "Book us a flight to Jamaica, Player," she added. "We've got to find that lost haven—and that treasure—before VILE does!"

CHAPTER 8

A Chartered Plane over the Atlantic Ocean

A S SOON AS THE PLANE TOOK OFF, CARMEN pulled out the diary. Finding that code had been a lucky break. Could there be other clues hidden in the dusty old pages?

"Next stop, Jamaica," Player said over the comm-link. "That's the fourth largest island country in the Caribbean Sea by population. There are almost three million people living there, but lots more come to visit—tourism is one of the island's biggest industries. People go there for its tropical weather, its beautiful beaches and waterfalls, and its reggae music."

"That last part sounds like Vile Island, minus the reggae," Carmen commented, flipping another page in the diary. "Professor Maelstrom is more of a grand opera kind of guy."

Zack helped himself to a handful of peanuts. "Opera? No wonder you left that place, Carm."

Carmen grimaced. Maelstrom's taste in music was the least of the reasons she'd left. As soon as she'd figured out that the criminal activity for which VILE was training her wasn't a game—that the group's heists actually hurt real people, innocent people—she'd known she had to get out. And to do whatever she could to stop them.

"Jamaica was settled by people from South America thousands of years ago," Player went on, "but Christopher Columbus claimed it for Spain in 1494. It was later taken over by British forces led by William Penn—that's the guy the state of Pennsylvania is named after. But the Spanish kept trying to get the place back, which is why the English governor eventually invited some buccaneers to settle in Port Royal. *Buccaneer* is just another word for pirate. He figured the pirates would help defend the island against Spanish attacks . . ."

After Player finished his briefing on their destination, Carmen forced herself to close her eyes and rest. It had been a long day and night, and she would need all her wits about her if she had to face Tigress again on the way to that treasure.

When she woke up, Zack and Ivy were snoring away

in their own seats, and nothing was visible outside the plane's window but open sea beneath a cloudless blue sky. Carmen checked her phone for the time — they'd been in the air for nearly eight hours, which meant they should be getting close. Luckily the time zones were working in their favor — while it was already getting on toward midafternoon back in London, they would be arriving in Kingston, Jamaica, at around 9:30 a.m. local time.

She picked up the diary and flipped it open to where she'd left off reading earlier. The next few entries were similar to the part she'd read before. Cal Cutlass talked about how great the other pirates were, how tough Captain Goldtooth was, how many doubloons they'd raided from a passing ship. She skimmed the next few entries, which mostly talked about Cal's daily life as a pirate, doing stuff like patching the sail, playing cards with his shipmates, and fishing for dinner.

A loud yawn came from across the aisle. "Where am I?" Zack mumbled. "Oh, hey, Carm. Are we there yet?"

"Quiet — I'm sleeping over here," Ivy complained with a groan.

"You guys should be landing in Jamaica pretty soon." Player's voice spoke out of Carmen's phone. "Better wake up and get ready to rumble. Tigress has a head start, remember?"

Carmen didn't need the reminder. Player was right —

they were going to have to hit the ground running. "Check it out," she said as she turned another page of the diary and a name near the top caught her eye. "Cal writes here about how he and the rest of Captain Goldtooth's crew just docked in Port Royal."

"Hey, that's where we're going!" Zack said, stifling another yawn.

"Yeah. Maybe this entry will tell us something useful."

"Read it to us, Red," Player said.

"Okay." Carmen cleared her throat and read aloud. "'On our way to Port Royal earlier this day, we encountered a merchant ship, which made various desperate attempts to evade our advances. However, Captain Goldtooth's bold and skilled crew soon drew alongside; "Prepare to be boarded!" rang out from various throats, mine included, and we swarmed the deck with our sabers held aloft. We must have been a fearsome sight, for the merchant crew surrendered immediately, offering no protest as we absconded with their goods and monies—and the captain's solid gold wedding ring for good measure! With such riches in hand, we were the toast of Port Royal this evening! I have never felt such camaraderie, joy, and freedom as I did then, singing, dancing, and feasting with my mates—even though I know that if they were ever to discover my true identity, I would be the one to face their wrath and most likely walk the plank! But luckily no one suspects a thing, and I have no plans to tell and give up the best adventure of my life. Who might have guessed that a farm girl from Yorkshire would become a terror of the high seas?'"

"Wait." Ivy sat up straight, suddenly looking wide-awake. "Did you say farm . . . *girl?*"

Carmen was already skimming back, wondering if she'd misread the faded, old-fashioned handwriting. But no . . .

"That's what it says," she said slowly as she skimmed ahead. "Whoa. Cal Cutlass . . . was a girl! She even goes on to say that Captain Goldtooth would allow no woman to set foot on his ship for fear of bad luck . . .'"

"Wait, what?" Ivy exclaimed, while Zack snorted with laughter.

Player spoke up. "Apparently that wasn't a rare opinion among pirates back then," he said. "I'm researching now, and a lot of pirate captains banned women and girls from their ships. But that doesn't mean there were no female pirates—a few famous ones were out and proud about it, like Anne Bonny, who sailed with the famous pirate Calico Jack. But others may have disguised themselves as men to join their crews."

"Like Cal Cutlass, apparently. Or Callie, or whatever her real name was." Carmen fingered the worn pages of the diary, imagining the girl-dressed-as-a-boy who'd written these words centuries ago. Somehow, knowing about Cal's grand deception made her story seem much more interesting. As a master of disguise herself, Carmen could appreciate the attention to detail it must have taken for Cal to keep her secret from a ship full of her fellow pirates 24-7. Too bad Cal had wasted those skills on a life of piracy and wrongdoing . . .

"Heads up, Red." Player's voice broke in to her thoughts. "Look outside—you're there."

Carmen leaned over and peered out the plane window. Far below, nestled like a green jewel in a sparkling blue sea, lay the island of Jamaica.

"Prepare for landing, guys," she said, reaching for her seat belt. "It's go time."

CHAPTER 9

Heathrow Airport

DEVINEAUX WAS IN LINE TO BOARD A PLANE AT Heathrow Airport when his phone buzzed in his pocket. He growled with irritation when he saw that it was Julia Argent—again.

"Yes?" he barked. "This is Devineaux."

"Oh, thank goodness, sir!" she exclaimed. "I've left you several messages—did you get them?"

Devineaux had, though he hadn't bothered to listen to any of them. He was sure she was calling merely to gloat about being asked to join the mysterious ACME only seconds after he'd received his own invitation.

"Er, of course I got them." He glanced toward the front of the line, where a stern-faced airline employee was poring over another passenger's ticket. "But I'm short of time, Miss Argent. What do you want?"

"I thought we should meet and discuss . . . well, you know . . . our new assignment?" She cleared her throat. "You left so quickly after they asked us to join that we didn't have a chance to talk. And ACME wishes to meet with us again as soon as possible."

"They will have to wait," he said. "You see, I received a new tip from one of our airport contacts that Carmen Sandiego flew out on a charter plane early this morning. I'm following up on it now."

"A tip?" Julia sounded a bit alarmed. "But you're not technically with Interpol anymore, and we also haven't technically started with ACME, so you really have no authority to . . . well . . . Wouldn't it be better to wait?"

"And let her slip through my grip yet again, only to cause yet more mischief and mayhem?" Devineaux barked out a dismissive laugh. "Nonsense. Besides, I haven't yet reached a decision about whether to accept that job offer, which means I might not leave Interpol after all."

"What? But ACME said they've already taken care of our transfers, sir, and even if you're still undecided, should you really be—"

"Look, it is none of your concern." Devineaux cut her off, annoyed by her goody-two-shoes attitude. It was always getting in his way! "If you prefer, Miss Argent, you can consider this my first freelance case." He smirked, liking the sound of that. "I don't need any help to bring down the notorious criminal Carmen Sandiego! Perhaps this is what I needed all along — to go rogue, just like her. It takes one to catch one, eh?"

Just then the airport's PA system crackled to life, announcing that the flight to Miami would be departing shortly, with connections to various stops in the Caribbean.

"I must go," Devineaux said abruptly. *"Au revoir,* Miss Argent. You can tell ACME that I'll be in touch with my decision once Carmen Sandiego is in custody."

Without waiting for a response, he hung up.

CARIBBEAN
ISLANDS

CITADELLE

CUBA

TORTUGA

HAITI

JAMAICA

DOMINICAN
REPUBLIC

PUERTO RICO

KINGSTON

PORT
ROYAL

CARIBBEAN SEA

CHAPTER 10

Off the Coast of Kingston, Jamaica

"CAN'T THIS THING GO ANY FASTER?" CARMEN asked Zack impatiently.

"Sorry, Carm. It's a beautiful morning, you know—all the better boats were rented out already." Zack gunned the motor on the small, somewhat rickety motorboat. They'd rented it at a marina in Kingston. Jamaica's bustling capital city hugged the shore on the southeastern coast of the island by Kingston Harbour, which Player had informed them was the world's seventh largest natural harbor.

"Yeah, this is the life." Ivy leaned back on the boat's rough wooden bench, her freckled face tipped up to catch the warm sunshine. "Why can't all our capers be in the Caribbean, huh?"

Carmen bit back a sigh. It really was a beautiful day in Jamaica. The sun glinted off the clear blue water of Kingston Harbour, a light breeze was blowing, and the temperature was perfect. Still, she couldn't enjoy the setting knowing how much was at stake—and how long it was taking them to reach the site of the sunken pirate city. She was pretty sure she would have made better time swimming!

But never mind—according to the coordinates Player had sent, they should be in the vicinity of old Port Royal by now. Up ahead, she could see the sandy strip of land called the Palisadoes, which separated Kingston Harbour from the Caribbean Sea. There was still a town called Port Royal there, though it was much smaller now.

As if reading her mind, Player spoke up in Carmen's ear. "If you're wondering about the part of Port Royal that's left, it's a shadow of its former self," he said. "Only about two thousand people live there, as opposed to eight thousand or so at the height of its reign as a pirate utopia."

"Well, we won't need to get too close to today's Port Royal—we should already be above the old pirate town," Carmen said. She reached for her oxygen tank and flippers as Zack brought the boat to a stop and Ivy opened her eyes and sat up. "You guys wait here—I'll dive down and see if I can get the lay of the land."

"Lay of the land—or lay of the water?" Ivy said with a grin.

Player spoke up again. "Remember, the clue said, 'Seek Morgan's stone,'" he reminded Carmen. "Sir Henry Morgan was a pretty big deal in Port Royal back in the day, so maybe there's a statue of him down there or something to mark where the treasure's buried."

"I'll see what I can find." Within seconds, Carmen was suited up in her scuba gear. When she was ready, she gave Zack and Ivy a thumbs-up and then tipped herself backwards off the side of the boat.

"Good thing Carm is the only one who knows how to scuba-dive, huh?" Ivy commented. "I sure wouldn't wanna have to swim down there—there might be sharks!"

"Don't worry, Carm can handle anything—even sharks, I bet." Zack leaned back in the driver's seat and tucked his hands behind his head. "Might as well work on my tan while we wait."

"Tan?" Ivy let out a snort. "You know you burn like a lobster if you spend more than five seconds in the sun, bro!" She jammed a wide-brimmed hat onto his head. "Do us all a favor and wear this."

Zack flicked the brim out of his face. "I wish you guys had let me stop and pick up some food before we left," he complained. "We walked right past at least three jerk-chicken stands back in Kingston!"

Ivy ignored him, leaning over the side of the boat and peering into the water. It was clear and tranquil, but too deep for her to see where Carmen might be. "I wish we could see what Carm's doing down there."

Zack grabbed a long tubular-shaped object from a compartment under the boat's wheel. "Here, try this," he said.

"What is that thing?" Ivy took it and peeked into both ends. "A telescope?"

"Pirates called it a spyglass—they used them for navigating and stuff," Zack said. At his sister's surprised look, he shrugged. "It was in that pirate show I saw."

Ivy peered through the spyglass. It didn't help much with seeing through the water. But when she raised it, she had a fantastic view of the area all around. She looked at the shoreline back in Kingston, able to see a fair bit of detail even though it was more than two miles away. "Hey, bro, I think I see one of those jerk-chicken shacks you were just talking about," she said. "Long line—must be good."

"Aw, man!" Zack exclaimed hungrily.

Then Ivy turned the glass in the other direction—and gasped. "Uh-oh," she said.

"What's wrong?" Zack asked.

Ivy gulped and handed him the spyglass. "Check it out. There's this big yacht coming this way."

"So what?" Zack said. "They'll have to go around us."

"Just take a look, bro."

Zack lifted the spyglass, focusing it on the white speck on the horizon. Through the lens, the speck turned into a big, beautiful yacht. He was admiring its clean lines and the way it sliced through the water when he noticed someone standing on the bow. Someone very familiar . . .

"Uh-oh!" he blurted out.

"Yeah," Ivy said grimly. "Tigress is on that yacht! And she's coming straight for us!"

"Let's get out of here." Zack tossed aside the spyglass. He didn't need it to get a good look at the yacht anymore, anyway—it was closing the distance between them like crazy! He sat up straight in the driver's seat and gunned the motor.

"What about Carm?" Ivy cried as the little motorboat lurched into motion.

"We'll come back for her later," Zack called back. "Hold on, sis!"

He spun the wheel, heading toward the shore of the nearby Palisadoes. Maybe he could get them to shallow water where that whale of a yacht couldn't follow . . .

"Faster, bro!" Ivy shouted, hanging on to the side of the boat. "They're still gaining on us!"

"Duh! That thing probably has, like, a thousand-horsepower engine," Zack said, yanking the wheel sharply to the left to try to regain some distance. "And here we are in this bathtub toy . . ."

Ivy cringed, hardly daring to look up at the yacht, which now seemed to tower above them. Zack turned to the right, aiming for an inlet in the Palisadoes, and for a second she thought he might actually make it . . .

CLUNK! The small boat suddenly slowed down. A lot.

"What was that?" Ivy cried.

"Motor died," Zack said. "Uh, anyone got a paddle?"

"Real funny, bro." Ivy turned to watch as the yacht glided to a stop just a few yards off the starboard side. Tigress wasn't alone now—three other figures stood beside her.

"Uh-oh," Ivy said, recognizing the hulking shoulders and spiky hair of one of the figures. "There's that El Topo guy."

"Yeah, and Le Chèvre, too," Zack added, pointing to a taller, leaner figure. "Who's the clown?"

Ivy shrugged. "Maybe VILE's doing birthday parties now."

On the yacht, the mystery clown guy with the white

makeup and striped shirt was jumping around, waving his arms in the air. "What's he doing?" Zack wondered.

Tigress was close enough to hear him by now. She smiled smugly. "Allow me to translate," she called out. "He's saying, 'Prepare to be boarded.'"

CHAPTER 11

C ARMEN KICKED WITH HER FLIPPERS, SENDING herself gliding through the murky undersea world. She was pretty deep here, probably almost forty feet down, but there was still just enough light filtering through from the surface to see pretty well.

"So this is the lost pirate haven," she said to Player, her voice sounding gurgly in her own head thanks to her face-mask. She glanced around at the ghostly shapes of skeletal buildings. "After more than three hundred years underwater, there isn't much left of old Port Royal."

"What can you see down there?" Player asked.

"There are still some walls and streets and stuff. Not

exactly the bustling city it used to be, though. It's almost a little creepy."

She paused to admire the stonework on a doorframe. Then she swam on, looking for anything that might be a hint to her quest.

"Can you see anything that might match up with those rock formations on the map?" Player asked. "Or any statues of Henry Morgan?"

"Not yet." Carmen kicked her flippers again, gliding over a crumbled stone wall covered in waving seaweed. "Just think, Cal Cutlass probably walked these streets before that earthquake sank them. I wonder what she thought of the place."

"Who knows," Player said. "Supposedly it was known as the most dangerous and depraved city in the world back then."

Carmen grimaced. "Sounds a little like Vile Island."

She kicked again, still thinking about Cal Cutlass. How crazy was it that the notorious pirate was a girl— and that nobody had figured that out until now? It made Carmen want to finish reading that diary once this mission was over. Maybe find out what had made Cal betray the captain she seemed to admire so much by stealing his treasure. Was it merely ordinary greed— the same kind of greed that had led her to become a pirate in the first place? Or could something else have happened . . . ?

Just then Carmen noticed several rows of rounded stones set into the sea floor ahead. They were covered in barnacles and worn down by hundreds of years of sea currents, but she was pretty sure she knew what they were.

"Gravestones," she blurted out.

"What was that, Red?" Player asked.

Carmen kicked down to the stones. "I found an old cemetery," she said. "Do you happen to know where Henry Morgan is buried?"

"Hang on, I'll check . . ." Player was silent for only a few seconds. "Actually, his grave is in Palisadoes cemetery in Port Royal, Jamaica." He sounded excited. "'Seek Morgan's stone . . .'"

"As in his gravestone?" Carmen was already swimming from one ancient grave marker to the next, using a flashlight from her pack to try to make out the names carved into them, which had been worn down but not yet totally erased. "Maybe the treasure is buried in his grave!"

"Ew—you up for some underwater grave digging, Red?"

"Not really." Carmen shone her light on another stone. "But a girl's gotta do what a girl's gotta—found it!"

She stared at the faded notation on a large stone: SIR HENRY MORGAN, 1635–1688.

"It's weird that the cemetery wasn't on the map," Player commented.

"Yeah. Weird." Carmen floated there for a moment, staring at the stone and thinking hard. "Something doesn't make sense here, Player. Cal Cutlass created the clue we're following. By the time she drew that map, she must have known that Port Royal was lost beneath the sea. So why would the map show a beach and trees and all the rest if the treasure site is underwater? And what does Henry Morgan's gravestone have to do with it?"

Player thought. "What if that clue isn't leading to the treasure at all? What if it's leading to . . ."

". . . another clue." Carmen smiled and shook her head. "Of course! Cal Cutlass went to all that trouble to steal the treasure—she wasn't going to make it easy to find, right?"

"Makes sense. So do you see anything that might be another clue?"

"Checking now." She ran her hands over the face of the grave marker, searching for any indentation where something could be hidden. When she found nothing, she moved to the back.

Finally her fingers found a grooved mark. But it wasn't a niche or hidey-hole. It was a carved symbol! No—a whole series of them!

"Found it!" Carmen's heart pounded with excitement.

"It's carved into the back of the gravestone—another coded clue, I think. I'll get some scans and send them to you when I'm back up top."

She pulled out her compact, clicking it open to reveal the optical scanner. She took several scans of the message, and close-ups of each symbol just to be safe. The names on the gravestones weren't the only things that were fading. The sea had been wearing down Cal Cutlass's carved symbols for hundreds of years too—Carmen didn't want to take any chances.

"Think Tigress has already been there?" Player wondered.

"No way of knowing," Carmen said, snapping one last image. "It's not exactly like she could take the gravestone with her."

"Ivy has the decoder, right? Get up there and see what we've got," Player said.

"On my way." Carmen tucked away the compact and flashlight and kicked for the surface. "Hey, Player, did a storm roll in while I was down here?"

"I don't see anything on radar. Why?"

"It got darker all of a sudden." Carmen glanced up. A very large, very dark shadow was blocking the bright sky above the surface of the sea. A ship? She didn't remember seeing any large vessels nearby when she'd started her dive. Then again, she'd swum a fair distance through the sunken city — she just hoped Zack and Ivy were keeping an eye out for her so she didn't have to swim too far to meet them . . .

Seconds later, she surfaced. Sure enough, she was in the shadow of an enormous yacht.

"Nice boat," she murmured, treading water.

"Huh?" Player said.

"Nothing." Carmen pulled off her mask and squinted into the bright morning sunlight, scanning the horizon for Zack and Ivy's little boat.

She didn't see it. But when she glanced up at the yacht, wondering if the little boat was hidden behind it, she gasped.

"Red? What is it?" Player asked.

"Tigress!" Carmen hissed. "She's here — and she's not alone! El Topo is with her, and Le Chèvre. Mime Bomb, too."

She was surprised to see so many operatives together. That wasn't the usual VILE protocol. Sure, El Topo and Le Chèvre were friends and often worked together. And occasionally Professor Maelstrom would send other operatives out in pairs for a particular mission. But a whole crew of them?

"Talk about a scary ship full of modern-day pirates," she murmured.

"Do they see you?" Player asked.

"Not yet. I can probably still get away before . . ." Carmen's voice trailed off, and she blinked seawater out of her eyes, wondering if she was seeing things. Because El Topo and Le Chèvre had just leaned a long, flat piece of wood over the side of the yacht, letting it hang out over the sea like a diving board.

Mime Bomb pranced to the edge of it, joining his hands together and wiggling like a fish, then raising both hands over his head and miming a dive. Carmen wrinkled her nose in confusion. Were the VILE operatives planning to go swimming?

Then she gasped as Zack and Ivy stepped into view. Tigress was smirking at them.

"In case you need another translation," Tigress said, her voice ringing out clearly over the open water, "Mime Bomb was just explaining that this area is known by the locals as Sharkbite Reef. And if you don't tell me where Carmen Sandiego is in the next five seconds, it's where I've decided you two are going to walk the plank!"

CHAPTER 12

Zack reached for Ivy's hand. It wasn't easy, since the villains had bound the siblings' wrists with thick, scratchy rope. But he managed to brush her fingertips with his own.

"This might be it, sis," he said.

"No way," Ivy replied as El Topo and Le Chèvre shoved them onto the board. "Carm will rescue us. You'll see."

Tigress smirked. "She'd better hurry," she said, strolling to the edge of the yacht and glancing down. "Because those sharks look hungry."

"Sh-sh-sharks?" Zack cried, staring down at the water far below. "No way! You can't throw me in the drink—I don't even like fish!" He gulped. Was that a ghostly shape he'd just seen gliding under the yacht? It looked a little small to be a shark, but what if he was wrong?

The weird-looking clown guy that Tigress kept calling Mime Bomb danced over, waving his hands around his face. "Huh?" Ivy said. "Speak up, dude."

"He's asking if you have any last words," Tigress said. "Perhaps a message for your friend Black Sheep—I mean, Carmen Sandiego?"

"Oh." Suddenly Zack had an idea. In movies, people were always stalling the bad guys by talking a lot. Maybe he could try that—he was good at talking! "Uh, actually, I do have something to say before I depart this life. But what is life, really? Just a lot of breathing and eating . . ." He paused as his stomach grumbled. "Oh, the eating! Listen, don't prisoners usually get a last meal request? Because I could really go for some good old Boston baked beans right now . . ."

Le Chèvre spoke up. "Let's get this over with, *oui*? We should already be on our way to—"

"Quiet," Tigress interrupted, glaring at him fiercely. "This won't take long. And it should keep you-know-who off our tail for a while." She flexed her claws. "Not that I'd mind taking her on again myself . . ."

"Oh, good," a voice said from atop the fly bridge. "Because I'm just itching for a catfight."

"Carm!" Zack cried.

At the same moment, Ivy kicked out at Le Chèvre, sending him tumbling over the edge of the board and into the water. "Take that, Goat Boy!" she cried.

"No!" El Topo exclaimed. "Hang on, *amigo*—I'll rescue you!"

He dove in. When Mime Bomb leaned over the edge to watch, Zack booted him in the rear end, sending him splashing down after the others.

Tigress didn't seem to notice what was going on with the rest of the operatives. She was totally focused on Carmen, who had just leaped down onto the deck. "Get ready to become shark bait just like your friends!" Tigress growled.

Then she leaped forward, landing a roundhouse kick on Carmen's shoulder. But Carmen came back just as hard with an elbow to the side.

"Yo, sis, untie me," Zack whispered, turning around so he and Ivy were back to back. "We can't help Carm if we're trussed up like Thanksgiving turkeys."

By the time Zack's hands were free, Tigress had backed Carmen up onto the plank. Tigress lunged forward, slashing with her claws at Carmen's face. Zack winced, then blew out a sigh of relief when Carmen dodged.

"Here, I'll do yours next," he told Ivy.

"Never mind that, bro," she said. "Think you can drive this thing?"

"Have you met me?" he exclaimed. "Like I've told you a million times, I can drive anything!"

"Good. Then get to the cockpit," she said. "And get ready to get us outta here!"

By then, Carmen was teetering at the far end of the plank. Tigress snarled in triumph and leaped forward to give her a shove over the edge.

But Carmen leaped off herself before Tigress could touch her — and caught the end of the plank with her fingertips on her way down. Tigress, surprised, went sailing forward right over Carmen's head, landing with a splash in the sea far below.

"Sorry," Carmen called down to her cheerfully. "I know cats don't like getting wet."

"Hurry!" Ivy cried, giving Zack a shove with her shoulder. "I'll help Carm."

But Carmen didn't need help. As Zack raced for the cockpit, he could already see her flipping herself back up onto the yacht. Then she leaned out over the edge.

"Later, guys," she called to the operatives flailing in the water below. "Nice day for a swim, huh?"

FIFTEEN MINUTES LATER, THE YACHT WAS IDLING IN the open water of the Caribbean. Carmen, Ivy, and Zack were lounging on deck chairs. Carmen's smartphone was on a table nearby, with Player on speakerphone. The compact scanner was in her hand.

"Sending you the scans, Player," she said.

Ivy leaned over, lowering her sunglasses for a better look at Carmen's phone. "That's the next clue?"

"Uh-huh." Carmen studied the line of symbols:

"Who has the decoder?" she asked.

"Right here." Ivy pulled it out. "First symbol?"

It took a few minutes to decode the message. The carvings were worn from hundreds of years spent under the sea. Carmen had to check the individual scans of each symbol to get a clear enough look at them. As she wrote down the final letter, Zack read the whole thing out.

"'Cave of brethren shows the way,'" he said. "What the heck does that mean?"

"I'm not sure," Carmen replied. "Player, any ideas?"

"Working on it," he said. "There are caves all over

Jamaica. Could Cal Cutlass's treasure be buried in one of them?"

"Maybe." Carmen gazed at the clue uncertainly. "But the map doesn't show a cave."

Zack groaned. "Oh no! Another puzzle?"

"Looks that way," Player said. "But hey, here's something—I just ran a search cross-referencing brethren, caves, and pirates, and it turned up an interesting result."

Carmen sat up straight. "What?"

"Tortuga!" Player said.

"Where?" Ivy said. "Wait—that sounds familiar . . ."

"That's because it came up last time," Carmen reminded her. "It's another old pirate haven, off the coast of Haiti."

"Right," Player said. "But this time it really might be the place we want. For one thing, there are a bunch of old caves on the island. But that's not all. See, back in the Golden Age of Piracy, there was this group called Brethren of the Coast. It was kind of like a union for pirates or something. And guess where the Brethren had their headquarters?"

Zack scratched his head. "Uh, New York City?" he guessed. "No, wait—Boston!"

"No, I've got it!" Ivy exclaimed. "It's gotta be this Tortuga place, right?"

"Exactly."

Carmen smiled. "Good work, Player. Zack, let's head to the airport. We're going to Haiti!"

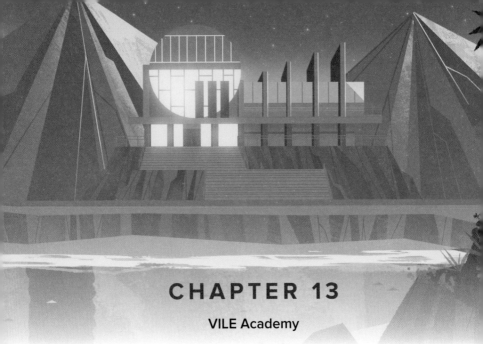

CHAPTER 13

VILE Academy

I
T'S NOT MY FAULT," TIGRESS SAID, GLARING OUT OF THE comm screen with her wet hair dripping in her face. "This so-called crew you stuck me with is totally incompetent! Trust me, I can handle Carmen Sandiego on my own!"

"The evidence suggests otherwise, Tigress," Professor Maelstrom said sternly.

He was in the lounge with the rest of the faculty. Tigress had just contacted them—finally—with an update on the mission. And the news wasn't good.

"So the student formerly known as Black Sheep—she has the clue." Shadowsan's voice was as cold as ice.

Tigress shrugged, picking a strand of slimy seaweed out of her hair. "I don't know. We didn't exactly have time to catch up on all the gossip. But what matters is that *I* have it—and that we already decoded it and figured out what it's saying." She sounded proud of herself. "Anyway, as soon as we get back to Kingston, we'll be on our way to Tortuga."

"What's taking you so long?" Coach Brunt asked. "You're burning daylight, missy!"

"We . . . uh . . . ran into a little problem with the yacht." Tigress grimaced, her eyes flashing fire. "We had to borrow a different boat, and it's not quite as . . . um . . . high-powered."

Just then Mime Bomb stuck his head into the shot in front of Tigress. He grinned and waved, then started moving his arms back and forth.

"What's he doing?" Dr. Bellum asked, looking up from her screen.

Countess Cleo leaned forward. "I think he's . . . rowing?" she said.

Maelstrom gritted his teeth. The lost pirate's treasure should be valuable enough to pay for all the heists that the Red Rogue had ruined over the past few months . . . if only they could beat her to it!

"This is ridiculous—Tigress, I expect you to make

this work!" he snapped. "We can't let Carmen Sandiego steal anything else out from under us!"

"Don't worry, we'll get there first," Tigress said. "You can count on it."

CHAPTER 14

A Chartered Plane over the Caribbean Sea

O KAY, LISTEN UP," PLAYER SAID AS SOON AS THE small plane took off from Kingston. "This flight from Jamaica to Haiti won't take long, since they're only around three hundred miles apart."

"Tell us what we need to know, Player." Carmen settled into her seat. "We won't have much time to get to know the place once we arrive. I have a hunch we're getting close to Cal's treasure. And we don't want Tigress to beat us to it."

"Tigress?" Ivy laughed. "Are you kidding? She'll be lucky if the sharks don't chew those claws of hers right off!"

"Never count out a VILE operative," Carmen warned.

Sure, the last time they'd seen Tigress she was floating in the open water with the rest of her crew. But Carmen knew that wouldn't stop the VILE gang for long. "Go ahead, Player," she added.

"So Haiti makes up the western part of a Caribbean island called Hispaniola," Player said. "The eastern part is the nation of the Dominican Republic."

"The Dominican Republic? Hey, that's where Big Papi is from!" Zack exclaimed.

"Who?" Carmen glanced at him.

"David Ortiz—he played for the Sox," Zack said. At Carmen's blank look, he shook his head. "The Boston Red Sox? As in, the world's greatest baseball team ever?"

"What, did you grow up on a deserted island or something, Carm?" Ivy exclaimed. Then she blinked. "Oh, wait . . ."

"Okay, back to Haiti," Carmen said, rolling her eyes. "More specifically, Tortuga."

"Right," Player said. "Tortuga's official name these days is the Île de la Tortue. It lies just off the northwest mainland of Haiti across the Canal de la Tortue. It was named by Christopher Columbus, who thought the island's shape looked like a turtle's shell—*tortuga* is Spanish for 'turtle.'"

"Forget Christopher Columbus," Zack said. "When do the pirates come in?"

"Around the 1630s," Player replied. "By 1640, the pirates of Tortuga were calling themselves the Brethren of the Coast. Tortuga was considered a stronghold of the buccaneers just like Port Royal—pirates set out on all kinds of raids from there. It was also known as a good place to hide pirate booty, or to sell it."

"Then it would make sense if Captain Goldtooth had hidden his treasure there," Carmen said. "And I bet Cal Cutlass knew that and stole it from wherever he'd hidden it! If so, it could still be on Tortuga. She wouldn't have wanted to try to transport it all over the place—that would only have given Goldtooth more time to try to find her and take it back."

"That would also explain why the booty hasn't been found yet," Player said. "There aren't a whole lot of people living on Tortuga even now—best estimate is around thirty thousand on the whole island. And there's hardly any tourism, either, even though the beaches are supposed to be beautiful."

"Weird," Zack said. "Who doesn't love a good beach?"

Ivy nodded. "Yeah. I mean, Carson Beach in Boston isn't even that nice, and it's crowded all the time!"

"And there are caves on the island?" Carmen asked Player. "Like the one in the clue, maybe?"

"Maybe. Like I said, the Brethren of the Coast were

known to hang out on Tortuga. And there are lots of caves in the mountains."

"'Cave of Brethren shows the way,'" Carmen murmured. "It doesn't sound like the treasure is actually in the cave, does it? Probably just another clue."

"Let's hope it's the last one," Player said. "As in, the one pointing us to the location on the treasure map."

Carmen nodded. "There might be more clues in here," she said, picking up the diary. "I think I'll keep reading."

"Let us know if you find anything interesting," Player said.

Carmen opened the diary to the spot where she'd left off and started to read. It could be difficult to make out some of the entries, since Cal's handwriting was sometimes messy and the ink often smudged or faded with age. At first Carmen wasn't sure it was worth the effort. There was more bragging, more boring talk about mending sails, and even an entire paragraph about how Captain Goldtooth had told Cal how cool her eye patch looked.

But then, a few pages later, the tone started to change. First Cal wrote about boarding a ship that had some families traveling to the New World.

"Oh, man," Carmen murmured as she read.

Ivy looked up from the game she was playing on her phone. "What? Did you find a clue?"

"Not exactly," Carmen said. "But I think maybe Cal

is starting to have doubts about being a pirate. She just wrote about how the crew attacked a ship with some little kids on it. The kids were scared of the pirates, and when they started to cry, Cal wanted to comfort them. But the other pirates chased them below deck and locked them in the hold." She shuddered. "Horrible, right?"

"Wow, pirates were mean," Zack said. "They always seem so happy on TV! Just having fun singing, drinking ale, making people walk the plank . . ."

Ivy rolled her eyes. "Yeah, sounds like a barrel of laughs."

Carmen was reading again. After skimming past a few more entries about thunderstorms, rats getting into the food stores, and Captain Goldtooth's broken sword, she spoke up again. "Okay, this is interesting—now Cal says they're heading back to Tortuga to restock their provisions."

"Tortuga?" Zack sat up straight in his seat. "That's where we're going!"

"Yeah." Carmen flipped to the next page and scanned it. "Oh, wow. It turns out Captain Goldtooth had no intention of shopping for provisions at the local trading post. Instead of landing at the pirate port, they sailed to a small village at the other end of the island. Listen, here's what Cal writes: 'Oh, it was horrible! The village was quite poor and the elders begged us to leave them in peace as they meant no harm to anyone. But that did not stop the captain from laying waste to what little they had. He ordered us crewmates to take it all—the dusty bits of grain in the bins, the freshly baked loaves cooling on the windowsills, every last goat and chicken, even the rough leather sandals off the villagers' feet! And when the captain deemed it so meager a bounty as to be an insult, he ordered us to burn the village to the ground!'"

Zack gasped. "Whoa, what a jerk!"

"Apparently Cal agreed," Carmen said. "She was having doubts already after the thing with the little kids. And this was the last straw. She finally realized being a pirate was about more than singing sea chanteys and having fun with your shipmates. And that stealing really does hurt people." She smiled wryly. "Sounds kind of familiar . . ."

Carmen's mind wandered back to the day she realized what VILE's true intentions were. Growing up there, for as long as she could remember, she'd always thought of stealing as a game. But once she knew the truth, and had seen what lengths VILE would go to in order to get the goods, there was no going back . . .

She shook off those memories and read on, wanting to know whether Cal Cutlass had made the same choice. Could that be the real reason she'd decided to steal Captain Goldtooth's treasure? Not for her own financial gain—but to try to foil the pirates she'd once considered family after she found out just how evil they were? Just like Carmen had done with VILE?

For the next few minutes, the only sounds in the plane were Zack's crunching as he worked his way through the plane's bags of pretzels and the beeping of Ivy's phone game. But Carmen didn't hear any of it. She was totally engrossed in Cal Cutlass's story as the young pirate vowed to make up for her past misdeeds as best she could. First she planned to steal and hide the captain's entire treasure. Then she would send the map and decoder to that poor Tortugan village so the people there would be the ones to find the treasure. As Carmen read through Cal's plans, she suddenly let out a laugh.

Ivy looked up from her game. "What's so funny, Carm?"

"It's Cal." Carmen smiled. "I like the way she thinks. She's planning to steal Captain Goldtooth's treasure, but she's not going to stop there. She wants to snatch his favorite hat, too—just to let him know how it feels to lose something special!"

"Uh, Red?" Player said. "You do realize these people all lived, like, three hundred and some years ago, right?"

Carmen smiled sheepishly. "I know. But they were real people, and I'm glad Cal realized the error of her ways, even if it took her a while." She shrugged. "She reminds me of me."

"Yeah, Cal Cutlass totally stuck it to those pirates," Zack said. "Just like you're always sticking it to VILE, Carm!"

Carmen touched the faded old pages of the diary. Suddenly it felt as if Cal Cutlass were right there with her, helping guide her quest. Carmen didn't want to let her down. "We definitely don't want Tigress to get to that treasure before we do," she murmured, talking more to herself than to the others. "Maybe we can still help Cal finish what she started."

Zack swooped his finger around the inside of an empty pretzel bag, then licked off the salt and crumbs. "What do you mean?"

"That treasure has never been found," Carmen said. "That means Cal Cutlass must not have had a chance to give the map and decoder to the villagers."

Player spoke up. "Right," he said. "She ended up in Newgate Prison in London, remember? Sentenced to hang at Execution Dock. That was a gallows located on the bank of the Thames where they hanged condemned people for, like, four hundred years. Lots of pirates took their last breaths there—even the super-famous pirate Captain Kidd!"

"Whoa!" Ivy sounded alarmed. "Is that what happened to Cal?"

"No," Carmen said. "You said she escaped from prison, right, Player?"

"Right. And was never heard from again."

Carmen nodded, thinking about what she might have done in Cal's place. "Since nobody knew she was a girl, she probably was able to live incognito after her escape."

"But I guess the people of Tortuga never got the treasure," Ivy said.

Carmen nodded, less concerned about how and why Cal's long-ago plans had failed than in how Carmen could take on Cal's quest as her own right now, today. Finish what the brave young pirate had started all those years ago. Make things right in any way Carmen could, just as she'd been doing ever since escaping Vile Island.

Ivy peered out the window. "Hey, I think I see it!" she cried. "That's gotta be Haiti down there, right?"

Carmen looked out too. "Right," she said, touching the diary once more.

We're coming, Cal Cutlass, she thought with a shiver. *And we'll help you put things right, or my name isn't Carmen Sandiego . . .*

CHAPTER 15

Port-de-Paix, Haiti

CARMEN'S CHARTER PLANE BYPASSED THE CAPITAL city of Port-au-Prince, landing instead in Port-de-Paix, the closest city to Tortuga. Soon Carmen, Ivy, and Zack were wandering through the dusty city. "Now what?" Carmen asked Player.

"I've been trying to research how to get to Tortuga, but it's not easy," Player said. "There's supposed to be a ferry, but I can't find much information."

"Wow." Carmen smiled. "Has the internet failed you at last, Player?"

"Funny, Red. I'll keep looking, but you might have to improvise this time."

"That's okay. I'm good at improvising." Carmen

glanced around. Across the street stood a pretty, white-washed church with blue trim, and beside that were several shops with colorful awnings to protect them from the intense Caribbean sun. One of the awnings had the tidy words TOURIST INFORMATION stenciled on it.

"Look!" Zack pointed to another shop. On this one, the awning read simply RESTAURANT. "Time for a late lunch?"

"You mean the four sandwiches and seven thousand pretzels you ate on the plane weren't enough?" Carmen raised an eyebrow at him, then strode off toward the tourist place. "Anyway, there's no time to waste on food," she called over her shoulder. "Let's see if we can start improvising."

Inside the shop, a slender woman in her twenties was perched on a stool paging through a magazine. She tossed it aside when Carmen and the others entered.

"May I help you?" she asked eagerly, her voice lilting with an island accent.

"I hope so," Carmen said. "We want to visit Tortuga. How do we get there?"

"Île de la Tortue?" The young woman slid off her stool and hurried over. "Oh, I can certainly help with that! I was born there, and my grandfather still lives there. In fact, I was just thinking of visiting him soon—I could go now and take you with me in my boat if you like? I wouldn't charge you much, since I'd be going anyway."

Carmen smiled. This must be her lucky day! "That would be great," she said. "I'm Carmen, by the way. This is Zack, and that's Ivy."

"I'm Sasha. Come—let's go now, before the tide turns."

"I THINK I'M SEASICK." ZACK LOOKED A LITTLE GREENISH as he climbed off the small sailboat and on to the lush, sun-warmed island of Tortuga some time later. Sasha had steered the vessel with the expertise of someone who'd been sailing all her life, but the waters of the channel had been rough and choppy.

"Yeah, you don't look good, bro." Ivy hopped onto the dock and looked around. "This place looks nice, though."

"Thank you." Sasha sounded pleased as she tied off the boat. "Most people don't think so, I'm afraid."

"Jungle, beach, sunshine—what's not to like?" Carmen waved a hand at the bucolic scenery.

Sasha sounded sad when she responded. "My island is very poor, and most who live here have little hope of a better life. If only the tourists would come, or if I could . . ." Her cheeks went pink, and she shook her head. "Ah, never mind."

"No—what were you going to say?" Carmen asked,

92

curious. For a second, she flashed back to Cal Cutlass's diary—and the attack on the Tortugan village that had soured Cal on a pirate's life. A village much like this one, perhaps?

"As I said, very few people come here," Sasha said. "My dream is that I could find a way to make them come—to show the world my beautiful island. You may not know, but once upon a time many famous pirates lived here . . ."

"Yes, I think I've heard something about that," Carmen said, trying not to smile.

"Well, it might be silly." Sasha ducked her head. "But I wish I could turn that history into a sort of resort. People would come to learn about the pirates, and perhaps they'd stay to enjoy the beautiful beaches and nature."

"Cool," Ivy said. "Like one of those . . . whaddaya call 'em . . . eco-resorts. But with pirates!"

"Exactly." Sasha sighed, then laughed. "As I said, it is silly. Where would I ever get enough money to do something like that?" She fingered the coins Carmen had paid her for the boat ride.

Carmen nodded sympathetically. But her mind was already returning to the quest. "Listen, do you happen to know if anyone else traveled here today?" She pointed from herself to Zack and Ivy. "Outsiders, like us?"

"I don't know. But I'll find out." Sasha hurried over

to an old woman seated on a stump nearby scraping the scales from a fish. Sasha spoke to her for a moment, then hurried back. "No—Miss Esterline says nobody has come today except a few locals. At least not through this port."

"Good." Carmen glanced inland, toward the mountains rising from the jungle. "So, Sasha, what do you know about this island's caves?"

"I used to play in some of them as a child," Sasha said. "Would you like to see them? I could take you there—it's only a short walk."

"Actually, we're looking for a specific cave." Carmen hesitated, not sure how much to tell her. Sasha seemed trustworthy, but a lifetime dealing with criminals had taught Carmen to be cautious.

"Yeah, the Cave of the Brethren!" Zack blurted out.

"Zack!" Ivy smacked him on the shoulder. "We're supposed to be undercover!"

Sasha glanced from one of the siblings to the other, her expression a little confused. "I don't know of any cave by that name," she said. "But my grandfather has lived here his whole life. He knows every square meter of this island. We could ask him."

"That would be great, thanks." Carmen shot Zack a dirty look but decided not to worry about his slip. She was pretty good at reading people—yet another skill she'd picked up during her years at VILE Academy—and Sasha definitely seemed like a good egg.

Sasha's grandfather was a very old, very wrinkled man with a gap in his teeth. He listened to their request thoughtfully from his seat on an overturned crate outside a humble hut in the village. "Cave of the Brethren, eh?" he asked, his accent stronger than Sasha's. "Yes, I know it. Nobody calls it that anymore, though. It was long known as a secret meeting place for some of the Brethren of the Coast, especially in the early days when the various captains often didn't trust one another much." He winked. "There may have been a pirate code back then laying out rules of conduct and fairness. But that doesn't mean everyone followed it. Some, like Blackbeard and Henry Morgan, were known to live by their ideals. Others?" He shrugged. "Well, it's said that Charles Vane was as quick to break the code as to follow it. Never mind even worse scoundrels, like Captain Goldtooth or François l'Olonnais."

"Wow, you know a lot about pirates!" Zack exclaimed.

Sasha smiled fondly at the old man. "Yes, he'd make the perfect tour guide for my imaginary resort, eh?" she joked. "Granpapa, can you tell them how to get to this cave?"

Her grandfather waved a hand toward the mountains. "It's that way," he pronounced. "But unless you can climb straight up a sheer cliff like a spider . . ." He winked at the visitors again. "Well, then you must take the long way around and up the crooked tree road."

Sasha looked worried. "I know the road he means," she told Carmen. "It's more of a goat trail than a proper road, though."

Her mention of goats made Carmen's mind flash to Le Chèvre and the other operatives. "I need to get there—as soon as possible," she said. "Are there any cars I could rent? Or maybe an all-terrain vehicle, if the road's not very good?"

"Yeah, I can drive anything," Zack bragged. "Anywhere, anytime!"

"Let me see what I can do . . ." Sasha hurried off.

Twenty minutes later, Carmen was feeling impatient. Sasha had been asking around among everyone she knew, but it seemed that motorized transportation was difficult to come by in her grandfather's village. "My cousin offers the use of his donkey, Wesley," she told Carmen helplessly. "I'm afraid that's the best I can do."

"Maybe we should just walk," Ivy suggested. "I mean, if we can't find a car, you-know-who probably can't either. And we've got a head start, right?"

"It would take a very long time to walk even to the base of the trail," Sasha warned. "And that mountain is very steep. As Granpapa said, one side of it is basically a sheer cliff, and the other side isn't much better."

A boy about five years old raced up to them, dressed only in faded cotton shorts. "Sasha, Sasha!" he cried, hopping up and down with excitement. "What about cousin Joseph's zoom-zoom machine?"

"Oh, I forgot about that!" Sasha snapped her fingers and grinned at Carmen. "Be right back . . ."

Ten minutes later, Zack was pouring the last few drops from a rusty gas can into a small, rickety-looking motorbike. "You sure you can drive this thing, Carm?" he asked. "Maybe we can both fit on it."

Ivy glanced at the bike dubiously. "Don't think so, bro. Carmen'll be lucky if that thing can carry her up the mountain, let alone trying to squeeze your big behind on there with her."

"I'll be fine, guys." Carmen climbed aboard. Sasha gave Carmen directions, and soon the motorbike was chug-chugging along the trail heading for the mountain.

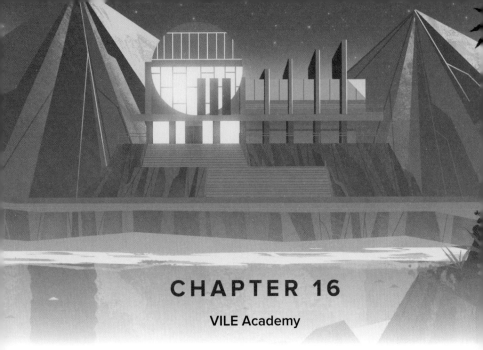

CHAPTER 16

VILE Academy

WELL, THIS IS UNWELCOME NEWS," PROFESSOR Maelstrom murmured, staring at the comm screen, which was flashing headlines from all over the world. He picked up a remote control and froze the screen, backing up until he found the article that had caught his eye.

Dr. Bellum looked up from her own virtual screen. "What? Did Tigress and her crew manage to do something else wrong?"

"No, nothing like that. They're finally on their way to Haiti as we speak." Maelstrom stroked his chin and stared at the news article. "But it seems an old pirate's diary was stolen from the Tower of London last night. The authorities are offering a reward for its safe return."

"Awfully coincidental, no?" Countess Cleo raised one perfectly groomed eyebrow.

"Maybe we should send out an operative to look for the diary." Coach Brunt's face twisted into a smirk. "We'll need that reward money if your precious Tigress fails to stop Carmen Sandiego."

"She won't fail," Maelstrom snapped. "But I wonder . . ." He let his voice trail off, feeling a twinge of unease.

"You wonder if Carmen Sandiego is the one who stole that diary?" Shadowsan frowned. "I'm wondering the very same thing myself."

"It doesn't matter." Maelstrom waved a hand to dismiss the matter. "As I said, Tigress and her crew are closing in on the treasure."

"Good." Countess Cleo stretched out an arm to study the rings she was wearing on every finger. "First dibs on the pirate booty," she said. "I could really use some new baubles."

CHAPTER 17

The Mountains of Tortuga

A COUPLE OF HOURS LATER, CARMEN GRIMACED AS the motorbike bounced over another stone in the steep, rocky, twisting trail up the mountain. It wasn't the first stone she'd hit—more like the hundred and first—but this time the bike landed with an unsettling hiss and clunk and the old-school bicycle horn attached to the handlebars let out a strangled squawk. A second later, the motor cut out with a *crunch*.

"Bad news," she said into her comm-link as she twisted the key and the engine grumbled reluctantly back to life. "I think my tire's busted. The engine isn't sounding too good either. Kind of a miracle it's lasted this long, actually."

That was the truth. Carmen was pretty sure the motorbike was older than she was, and that was being generous. The handlebars were rusted, the engine let out a funny little *ping* every few seconds, and the tires were all but bald.

"Never mind, Red," Player said. "You should be almost there."

"Good." Carmen peered ahead. "At least a good friend called gravity should help me getting back down—as long as the tires don't actually fall off this thing." Just ahead, a tree had fallen across the path. "I'm going to hoof it from here."

She climbed off the motorbike and grabbed the bag that held her trench coat and other tools. It was way too hot to wear anything more than the shorts and T-shirt she had on, so she just slung the bag over her shoulder and set off. She hopped over the fallen tree and followed the trail up a steep hill and around a large boulder. As she rounded the corner, she stopped short, startled by the sight of the ground disappearing in front of her.

"Now I know what Sasha's Granpapa was talking about," she said, peering over the edge of a sheer cliff, dotted with only a few scrubby plants and protruding rocks between where she was standing and the jungle floor nearly a thousand feet below.

"What was that?" Player asked.

"Never mind. Still looking for the cave." She edged past the drop-off and continued up the steep trail, keeping a sharp lookout for any signs of a cave. Even so, she almost missed it — if a bird hadn't flown out at that moment, she might never have spotted the dark opening hidden behind a tangle of vines.

"I think I found it," she told Player, pushing aside the foliage. "I'm going in."

She stepped into the cave, guided by the thin beam of her flashlight. The cave entrance was narrow and low, but after a few yards it opened up into a large, high-ceilinged chamber. Carmen swung the light around, checking out the rocky walls and rough floor, trying to imagine a group of pirates huddled around a fire . . .

She forgot about that when the flashlight beam caught a marking on the back wall. Carmen hurried closer.

"I found something," she told Player. "I think it's the clue!"

She pulled out her compact and scanned the coded message. Even in the dim light of her flashlight, she recognized several familiar symbols:

"Got it," Player said. "Who has the decoder?"

"Oh." Carmen realized the little round device was in the pocket of her coat. "Me. Hang on a sec . . ."

She took out her cellphone and snapped a photo. Then she hurried out of the cave, squinting to prepare herself for the strong afternoon sun after the dark cave.

"Don't leave us hanging, Red," Player said. "What's it say?"

"Working on it." Carmen perched on a boulder, propping the cellphone on one knee so she could see the picture she'd taken. Then she dug the decoder out of her bag. "I'll read out each letter and you write it down, okay?"

"Sure."

Carmen glanced at the phone, then spun the wheel of the decoder. "Okay, the first letter is a W . . ."

She kept going until she'd done the whole thing. Then Player read it back.

WEST POINT
EIGHTY PACES
SW FROM HEART
ROCK

"I'm guessing 'west point' could refer to the western-most point of the island—there's a beach there that looks like a pretty good match for the one on the map," Player said. "It'll be dark in a couple of hours but there's probably still time for you to—"

"Carmen Sandiego—halt where you are!" a voice cried out, drowning out the rest of Player's comment.

Carmen leaped to her feet as Chase Devineaux stepped into view, red-faced, rumpled, and sweaty. "Whoa," she said, startled. "What—how—where'd you come from, Inspector?"

"I will ask the questions, *s'il vous plaît*," he retorted. "I must demand that you cease your plans to set up a crime headquarters on this island."

Carmen blinked, still trying to figure out how in the world Devineaux had tracked her down on this desolate mountaintop. The last time she'd seen him, he'd been flailing in the Thames—with no way of knowing where she was heading next.

"A crime headquarters?" she said. "What are you talking about?"

"It is no use lying to me, Carmen Sandiego. Interpol has eyes and ears everywhere—including airports all over the world. And of course, I am still a top Interpol agent —at least as far as most of those eyes and ears know at this moment." He smirked.

Carmen had no idea what he was talking about. But it didn't matter. She had to lose him, fast. There was no time to waste if she wanted to beat the VILE operatives to the treasure. "Whatever," she said. "If your eyes and ears think I'm setting up a crime HQ here"—her gaze swept over the steep jungle landscape—"they're sadly mistaken."

Devineaux shrugged and pulled out a handkerchief to mop his brow. "Fine—you will have plenty of time to confess once I take you into custody."

"I don't have time for this." Carmen pocketed the decoder and her phone, then grabbed her bag. "I have to go."

"No—stop right there!" Devineaux cried, lunging toward her.

Carmen dodged him easily, running down the trail and skidding around the corner by the sheer drop-off. For a second she thought about digging her glider out of her bag and taking a shortcut down. But she could already hear Devineaux crashing through the brush only steps behind her — there was no time.

Guess that'll teach me to keep my tools ready, even when it's hot, she thought ruefully.

She leaped over the fallen tree near where she'd left the motorbike. Right beside the bike, nibbling on the jungle foliage, stood a stout spotted donkey.

"Let me guess," she said. "You must be Wesley."

The donkey looked up at its name, blinking at her.

"Red?" Player said. "What's going on? Was that really the Interpol guy you were just talking to?"

"Crazy, right?" Carmen gave Wesley a quick pat. "Luckily even my half-broken-down motorbike should be faster than his mode of transportation. No offense, Wesley."

"Wesley? Who's that?" Player sounded confused.

"I'll explain later. Tell Zack and Ivy to stand by — we're going to the beach." Carmen leaped onto the motorbike and turned the key. The motor choked and sputtered, then finally roared to life.

She started down the trail at top speed, then glanced back over her shoulder. Devineaux was clambering awkwardly onto Wesley's back. The donkey's ears went flat with annoyance as Devineaux kicked him stoutly with both heels, shouting commands in French and bouncing around like a sack of potatoes when Wesley lumbered into a trot.

"That was close," Carmen told Player. "But I should be able to outrun—hey!"

Suddenly the motorbike started wobbling wildly, veering back and forth across the path despite her best efforts to steer. Out of the corner of her eye, Carmen saw something pop out from one of the tires, then another.

"Red? You okay?"

"Not exactly." Carmen fought to keep the bike upright as she throttled down. "Devineaux must've loosened my lug nuts! The rat!"

She wrestled the bike to a stop just as one of the tires popped off completely and rolled away down the hill. A second later came the sound of thudding hooves. Wesley trotted into view with Devineaux clinging to him, bouncing higher with each stride.

"Aha!" Devineaux called in triumph as Wesley drifted to a halt and stretched his head down to nibble at some grass. "Now I have you right where I want you, Carmen Sandiego. Will you come peacefully, or must I resort to using force?"

"Hmm, let me think about that . . ." Carmen tapped her chin, pretending to ponder the question. Meanwhile she was reaching for the old rubber bulb of the bicycle horn on the motorbike, hoping it still worked . . .

SQUAAAAAAWWWKKK!

The blare of the horn was so loud that Carmen jumped, even though she was expecting it.

Wesley, on the other hand, clearly hadn't expected it. He leaped up with all four hooves off the ground, braying in surprise.

"Stop that, you wretched beast!" Devineaux cried as the donkey spun around. The inspector grabbed for the creature's reins, but it was no use — Devineaux tipped off and landed on the rocky ground with a grunt and a splat.

The donkey leaped forward a few steps, then stopped again. He flattened his ears when Carmen vaulted onto his back. But he moved off obediently when she squeezed with her legs.

"Giddyup, Wesley," she said. "I bet you can run faster than some French guy, right?"

He could. When Carmen gave him another squeeze, Wesley stepped into a surprisingly smooth canter. "Noooo!" Devineaux cried, lurching to his unsteady feet. "That is *my* donkey!"

"Sorry, Inspector." Carmen waved cheerfully as the Interpol agent staggered after her, waving his fists. "I guess you can add donkey hijacking to my long list of crimes."

She was still laughing at her own joke when Devineaux's shouts of fury faded behind her.

CHAPTER 18

Just off the Coast of Tortuga

"Are we there yet?" Zack moaned, clinging to the side of Sasha's sailboat.

"Almost," Player said on the comm-link. "You'll be coming up on the westernmost point in a few minutes. Might want to bring the boat in now, though — the surf is higher up ahead, and I'm not sure Zack's stomach will hold out."

"Thanks, Player," Carmen said. She glanced at Sasha. "You can bring her in right here if that's okay. We'll walk the rest of the way."

"Sure." Sasha adjusted the rudder. "Who's Player? And how are you talking to him?"

"Uh, long story." Carmen traded a look with Ivy and Zack. "We'll tell you later."

Or maybe not, she thought, feeling a twinge of guilt. Without Sasha and her grandfather—and her cousin Joseph, for that matter—it might have taken much longer to track down that last clue. Carmen didn't want Sasha to feel used and kept in the dark, but there were some things she just didn't need to know.

Carmen pulled out her cellphone and handed it to Sasha. "We'll call you on this when we need you to come pick us up," she said. "We . . . uh . . . might need help loading something heavy."

Sasha looked confused. "Okay . . ."

Soon Carmen, Ivy, and Zack were on a wide strip of white sand separating the crystal blue water from the lush green jungle. The warm late-afternoon sunlight cast long shadows across the beach from several large, craggy outcroppings, ranging in size from a few meters tall to one the approximate size and shape of an eighteen-wheeler truck. Just beyond the rocks, a stream wound its way down the sand to meet the sea, with a line of swaying palm trees and other greenery lining both sides.

"Cool rocks," Ivy commented, squinting at them.

"Yeah, this whole place is nice!" Zack exclaimed, hoisting the shovel he was holding onto his shoulder. Ivy was carrying a spade as well, though she was using it as a walking stick.

Carmen barely spared a glance for the scenery. She was striding north along the beach, scanning the trees beyond the sand. "Look! Over there — that must be Heart Rock."

She pointed to a medium-size heart-shaped outcropping at the edge of the jungle. "Yeah." Zack gulped loudly. "And look over *there!*"

Several people were gathered in the middle of the beach up ahead, just a few meters beyond the largest rocky outcropping. "Tigress and her crew," Carmen said. "Looks like El Topo is already making progress on digging."

"Oh no!" Ivy looked worried. "What do we do now?"

"Yeah — they're winning!" Zack sounded just as upset as his sister.

"Don't worry, guys, we're still in this game." Carmen smiled at them. "Because I've been thinking about that last clue, and I realized something important. So here's what we're going to do . . ."

CHAPTER 19

Ten Minutes Later . . .

CARMEN CREPT ACROSS THE SAND TOWARD HEART Rock. She was almost there when Tigress spotted her.

"Well, if it isn't the Red Rogue!" she cried. "Late to the party as usual!"

"Let me guess." Carmen crossed her arms over her chest. "Le Chèvre scaled that cliff to beat me to the clue."

She'd figured it all out during the long ride down the mountain on Wesley. Le Chèvre could climb just about anything—even if Tigress's crew had arrived on Tortuga an hour or two after Carmen, he easily could have beat her up that mountain.

"Uh-huh. And it turns out Mime Bomb actually is

pretty good at cracking those codes. He figured it out right away." Tigress smirked, unsheathing her claws. "I told the faculty they didn't have to worry about you beating us to the treasure. But they always overestimated you—especially Shadowsan."

Carmen let out a snort. "Yeah, right!" She circled Tigress warily, staying just out of range. "That's why I failed his final exam and he wouldn't let me retake it, huh? Because I was teacher's pet?"

"Whatever." Tigress sounded bored. "The point is, I win. El Topo should have that pirate booty dug up any second now."

"Not if I find it first!" Carmen exclaimed. She leaped forward, darting around Tigress and circling the massive truck-size rock standing between her and where El Topo was digging steadily into the sand. Zack and Ivy had just darted out of the jungle and disappeared behind that same huge rock, though Carmen was pretty sure the VILE operatives hadn't noticed.

"Hey!" Tigress chased her. "Le Chèvre—a little help here?" she cried.

Le Chèvre rushed over, blocking Carmen's way before she could get halfway to El Topo's hole. "Stop right there!" he exclaimed.

Carmen rolled into a somersault, knocking his legs out from under him. Tigress growled and leaped forward, tackling Carmen in turn. Her claws slashed, barely missing their mark as Carmen rolled out from under her.

"Two against one?" Carmen taunted as Le Chèvre jumped to his feet and Tigress circled for another attack. "I always knew you guys were bullies."

"You're the bully, Carmen," Tigress sneered. "You're jealous because you couldn't hack it as a VILE operative. So you're trying to get revenge."

"You're half-right." Out of the corner of her eye, Carmen spotted Le Chèvre rapidly scaling the front of the truck-shaped rock. She jumped aside just as he leaped down toward her.

"Oof!" He landed in the sand. Carmen jumped over him and took off toward El Topo again. Mime Bomb was standing by the edge of El Topo's rapidly growing hole, watching the fight and shadowboxing along.

"Stop that!" Tigress yelled at him. "If you're not going to help us, at least help him!" She frowned as she glanced toward El Topo, who had all but disappeared into his hole. "How deep is this treasure buried, anyway?"

Mime Bomb shrugged dramatically. Then he pretended to pick up a shovel and mimed scooping sand out of El Topo's hole.

Carmen barely spared the diggers a glance. Tigress and Le Chèvre were already coming at her again . . .

For the next few minutes, the two operatives did their

best to stop her from reaching El Topo's digging site. Carmen battled her way closer and closer but was still several yards away when El Topo suddenly popped up out of the hole.

"The treasure is not here. It can't be!" he exclaimed. "I have already dug down thirty feet!"

Carmen snuck a look toward the little stream nearby. Was that a flash of movement behind the palm trees? She hoped so—she wouldn't be able to distract Tigress and the others much longer.

Le Chèvre scratched his head, looking confused. "We are digging in the right spot—I know it!"

"Oh, really?" Carmen smiled, pausing for a long moment to give Zack and Ivy a little more time. "I know something that VILE doesn't know," she singsonged playfully at last. "You measured out eighty paces from the heart-shaped rock, right?"

"Of course." Le Chèvre drew himself up to his full height. "I paced it out myself."

Carmen nodded. Zack and Ivy had reached the water's edge, the waves splashing against their legs and the pirate chest. El Topo had gone back into his hole, and sand was flying up from it again. Mime Bomb was peering down at his fellow operative.

"Yes, it makes sense that they'd have you pace it out, because your paces are probably close to those of a typical pirate," Carmen told Le Chèvre. "A typical *adult male* pirate, that is. But what you didn't know is that Cal Cutlass was *not* a typical adult male pirate."

Tigress frowned. "What are you talking about?"

"Cal was a teenage girl, not an adult man," Carmen said. "It's all in her diary—which I read, and you didn't." She smirked. "So her paces? They were probably a good five or six inches shorter than a man's."

Tigress's eyes widened as she caught on. "We were digging in the wrong spot!" she cried.

Mime Bomb suddenly raced over and tapped Tigress on the shoulder.

"What is it?" Tigress growled, pausing midcharge. "Get out of the way! I almost clawed your painted face off!"

Mime Bomb waved his arms and pointed frantically. Carmen backed away from Tigress, keeping a wary eye on Le Chèvre. But he was watching Mime Bomb now too.

"What are you saying?" Tigress exclaimed, sounding frustrated. "Three words—first word . . . uh . . . eyes?"

Mime Bomb had formed spectacles with his hands, peering through them in the direction of the huge truck-size outcropping. "Glasses?" Tigress guessed. "Goggles? Sightseeing? Oh, look, if you're going to . . ."

She trailed off. At her last few words, Mime Bomb had suddenly started dancing around and touching his nose.

"What'd I say?" Tigress asked Mime Bomb. "'Look'? Is that what you're trying to say? Look at what?"

This time Mime Bomb raised his arms and waved them around, keeping his legs close together. Tigress stared at him blankly.

"What?!" she exclaimed. "Why can't you just talk already?"

"I know!" Le Chèvre grinned. "He is pretending to be a tree!"

"A tree?" Tigress frowned. "What's that supposed to— oh! Is that what you're saying? 'Look at the tree'? Which tree?"

Le Chèvre glanced around. When he looked toward the palm trees, his eyes widened. "*Those* trees!" he cried.

"Heads up, guys!" Carmen shouted. "Incoming!"

She sprinted toward the palms by the stream. Just beyond the tree line, Ivy and Zack were dragging a battered wooden chest into the surf.

"Got it, Carm!" Ivy cried in triumph.

"Oh, man, this thing is heavy!" Zack groaned.

Tigress and Le Chèvre raced after Carmen. Le Chèvre skidded to a stop, and his jaw dropped. "Is that . . ." he began, staring at the wooden chest as Zack and Ivy pulled it farther into the water.

"Stop them!" Tigress yelled.

Carmen acted fast, flicking her wrist to shoot out her

grappling hook. It zipped across the sand at waist height, catching on a crag on one of the smaller outcroppings between the operatives and the sea.

"Oof!" Tigress grunted as she hit the rope, flipping head over heels onto the sand. "Ow!" she cried as Mime Bomb landed on top of her. "Get off me!"

Le Chèvre managed to skid to a stop just in time. He leaped over the rope, calling for help from El Topo, who was still deep in his hole, oblivious to everything else.

But by then Carmen was running through the surf to help Ivy and Zack. "Did you call Sasha?" she cried as she helped hoist the chest above the waves, which were splashing around their waists by then.

"Uh-huh." Zack nodded toward the deeper water. A sailboat was bobbing just beyond the breakers.

By the time the VILE operatives splashed into the surf, Carmen and her friends were almost to the sailboat. "Don't bother chasing us, Tigress," Carmen called as Sasha reached down to help haul the chest onto the boat. "I know cats don't like getting wet—especially twice in one day."

Tigress let out a yowl of frustration, but it was too late. Seconds later the sailboat was tacking back out to sea.

On the boat, Zack was already looking a little seasick. But he patted the top of the chest. "Come on, let's see what's inside!" he urged.

"What is that thing?" Sasha asked, glancing over as she went about her business sailing the boat.

"Oh, just your basic long-lost pirate booty," Ivy said casually. "It's all in a day's work for our girl Carmen."

Sasha looked confused, but Carmen nodded. "Let's see if all this was worth it."

She kneeled before the chest and pulled out an eyeliner pencil. Sasha looked confused.

"You're putting on makeup—now?" she said. "Are we going to a party?"

Carmen chuckled and flicked off the top of the pencil, revealing her lock-picking tool. The pirate chest's lock was rusty and stiff with age, but within seconds she had it open.

"Voilà," she said, flipping open the lid.

"Whoa!" Ivy whispered in awe.

For a long moment, nobody else said a word. They just stared at the treasure glinting in the light of the setting sun. Red rubies. Glittering green emeralds. Jewels of every shape and color, many set into intricate gold filigree rings, elaborate tiaras, or other jewelry. And then there were the doubloons—lots and lots of gold doubloons. Sitting on top of it all was a moldy old hat and a black eye patch.

Carmen smiled. "She did it," she said. "She even snagged Captain Goldtooth's favorite hat—just like she vowed." She reached out to touch the eye patch. "And this must have been hers . . . She wouldn't have needed that kind of disguise anymore, I guess."

Suddenly Zack found his voice. "Shiver me timbers!" he shouted. "Now, *this* is what I call pirate's booty!"

CHAPTER 20

L AND HO," Ivy cried as the docks of Port-de-
Paix drew closer. Sasha had steered the sailboat
straight back to mainland Haiti at Carmen's request.

"Are you ever going to tell me what just happened?"
Sasha asked as she adjusted the sail.

"Probably not." Carmen smiled ruefully. "Sorry. But
I'll make it up to you — promise."

"Okay, sure." Sasha eyed her warily but didn't say anything else as she steered the boat to shore.

Soon the trio was loading the treasure chest into the
trunk of a battered old taxi. "What if those VILE goons
come after us?" Zack asked, glancing nervously over his

shoulder. "It won't take them long to figure out where we went."

"Don't worry," Player said in Carmen's comm-link. "The plane's waiting. Engine's already running."

"Cool." Carmen told Zack and Ivy what Player had said. "Let's take separate taxis to the airport." She waved to hail a second cab idling nearby, then jumped into the first one. "I'll meet you two there. I have one last little errand to run on the way . . ."

CHASE DEVINEAUX CURSED IN FRENCH AS HE TRIPPED over yet another tree root. It was growing dark, and his progress down the treacherous mountain trail on foot was slow and rather painful. He'd tried to repair the motorbike, but after a long, sweaty search for that loose tire, he'd finally spotted it—only to have a large monkey suddenly appear and grab it, chattering wildly at him as it leaped up and disappeared into the treetops with the tire.

"Curse you, Carmen Sandiego," he muttered. "Curse you and the donkey you rode out on!"

Suddenly he became aware of a distant thrumming sound—a motor? He stopped and tilted his head, trying to figure out where it was coming from. Overhead? Could it be a passing small plane or helicopter? If so, perhaps he could flag it down—perhaps there was even time to catch up to Carmen Sandiego before she slipped completely through his fingers once again . . .

He hurried into a clearing and glanced up, but accidentally looked directly into the setting sun. Cursing again, he squeezed his eyes closed, certain now that the thrumming sound was coming from the sky just overhead.

Then he jumped as something clattered to the jungle floor nearby. He opened his eyes and stepped toward it, surprised to see a sleek, modern-looking polished metal cylinder with a tiny parachute attached to it.

"No monkey threw that at me," he said, squinting up at the sky again. But the thrumming had already faded, and there was no sight of an aircraft. "What in the world . . ."

He picked up the item. It appeared to be a container of some sort. When he twisted one end, a lid popped off, revealing something inside . . . A fountain pen!

Devineaux's jaw dropped when he saw the ACME logo on the pen. When he clicked the top of the pen, a glowing blue hologram burst out in full 3-D. It was Chief—the head of ACME, and his potential new boss.

"Enjoying your nature walk, Inspector Devineaux?" she asked with a quirk of one eyebrow. "I never took you for the outdoorsy type."

Devineaux let out a snort. "Are you going to crack jokes, or are you going to send someone to rescue me?"

"Why would I do that?" Chief replied. "You seem to have things under control."

Devineaux grimaced. "I did!" he insisted. "It was Carmen Sandiego—I had her! But she stole my donkey, and—"

"That's enough!" Chief cut him off. "Mr. Devineaux, this is not a game. If we invite you to join ACME . . ."

"*If?*" Devineaux exclaimed. "But you *have* invited me! Haven't you? You cannot go back on your word!"

"And *you* cannot go running off at the drop of a certain red hat," she said sternly. "You're lucky Agent Argent is sharp enough to figure out where you went. She also put in a good word for you, though I'm still not entirely convinced you're worth the trouble. Perhaps I should leave you to your . . . er . . . freelance work after all." The hologram shimmered and began to fade.

"No, please, I am worth it!" Devineaux cried, clutching the pen and clicking it again and again. "Upon my honor, madam, I swear I will do better! I shall never go rogue again, I promise! Don't leave me out here! I want to join ACME, I do!"

Chief smiled, still fading. "I thought you'd see things my way . . ."

A second later, Devineaux heard that thrumming

sound overhead again. A helicopter came into view, hovering over the clearing. Then a rope ladder tumbled down, nearly hitting him on the head. Devineaux grabbed it gratefully.

"Look out, Carmen Sandiego," he muttered, surveying the island as the chopper lifted him above the tropical canopy. "Perhaps I could not catch you as an Interpol agent. But things will be different now! I will find you, mark my—*mon Dieu!*" He cut himself off as a colorful jungle bird flew up past his face, squawking wildly—and deposited a moist white smelly blob directly on his head.

AT THAT VERY MOMENT, SASHA STEPPED INTO THE Tourist Information shop, gloomy now in the rapidly fading light. She sighed and looked around the shabby little room, still thinking back over the excitement of the past several hours, since the mysterious girl named Carmen had first walked in. What had just happened, anyway? Carmen and her friends had seemed nice enough, but that treasure . . . Sasha hoped she hadn't just helped a thief steal something that belonged rightfully to her island!

"Ah, well, it's back to normal now, in any case," she murmured, imagining days spent sitting here, perhaps occasionally being hired to transport someone to Île de la Tortue or down the coast to other beaches. Daydreaming all the while of something more — just as she'd always done.

She stepped behind the counter to turn off the light. As she did, she banged her foot on something wedged back there.

"Hey!" she exclaimed. "What is . . ." Her voice trailed off, and she gasped.

It was the treasure chest! She dropped to her knees, running her hands over its rough lid. Holding her breath, she swung the lid open — and fell back at the sight of all those jewels and doubloons, which somehow seemed to shine even more brightly in the dimly lit shop than they had under the Caribbean sun . . .

Lying atop the treasure was a folded sheet of white paper. Sasha picked it up and unfolded it with trembling hands.

Hi, Sasha,

Sorry I couldn't tell you everything. But I'm hoping this will make it up to you. It should be enough to get your eco-resort started — and fulfill your dream of making life better for all the people of Tortuga. Maybe that will help right some wrongs committed long ago. Good luck!

Your friend,
Carmen

Sasha stared at the words until she couldn't see them anymore because of the tears flooding her eyes. "Oh, thank you, Carmen!" she cried, clutching the note to her chest. "Thank you, thank you, thank you!"

"You *WHAT?!*" Zack cried as the plane banked over Haiti, heading east.

"What do you mean, you gave Sasha the treasure?!" Ivy exclaimed at the same time.

"Cal Cutlass always intended for that treasure to go to the people of Tortuga. And now it has," Carmen reminded them. "Besides, I always donate what I steal from VILE to a worthy cause, right? And what's a worthier cause than letting Sasha make her dream of helping her people come true?"

"I guess." Zack scowled. "But at least you coulda let us, you know, enjoy it for a few days."

"*Play* with it, you mean?" Ivy smirked at her brother. "Grow up!"

"You grow up!" Zack stuck out his tongue at her.

"Settle down, both of you," Carmen said. "Player, can you ask the pilot to take us back to London?"

"Already did," he said. "I figured you'd want to return that diary as soon as possible."

"You didn't give Cal's diary to Sasha for her pirate resort?" Ivy asked.

"I didn't want to get her in trouble for harboring stolen property," Carmen explained. "But don't worry, I'm planning to scan the whole thing on our way back and send it to her. She should know the whole story about Cal Cutlass—and why it's so important that the treasure stayed on Tortuga."

Zack nodded and sighed sadly. "I guess that's the end of our pirate adventure."

Carmen laughed. "Don't look so glum," she said. "What—you thought I wouldn't get a souvenir for you guys?" She reached into her trench coat and pulled out a couple of doubloons. "Here—catch!"

Zack cried out with delight as he caught his doubloon. Ivy grabbed hers, too, and studied it.

"Cool," she said. "Thanks, Carm."

"You're welcome. I'm sure Cal Cutlass would've wanted you to have them." Carmen pulled out one last item. "And I think she might've wanted me to hang on to this." She slipped on Cal's eye patch and struck a pose, hoping that somewhere, somehow, the brave female pirate was at rest now. "Jaunty, right? Maybe I'll be able to use it in a disguise sometime."

AT THE TRAITOR'S GATE: THE TOWER OF LONDON

Did you know . . .

* The original structure, the White Tower, was built by William the Conqueror in the 1070s.

* Its buildings and grounds have had many uses over the years, from prison to execution site, palace to arsenal, and zoo to royal mint.

* Queen Elizabeth I was once held prisoner there (before she was crowned) by her sister, Mary.

* Millions of people visit each year.

* It's not actually a single "tower," but a castle and fortress made up of numerous towers.

* The current buildings take up a full eighteen acres.

* The British Crown Jewels are kept at the Tower of London, where they are on display for visitors, and are among the most popular attractions in London.

* The Yeomen Warders, or "beefeaters," who guide tours there are a detachment of the Yeomen of the Guard, which was formed in 1485.

* Beefeaters are members of the Armed Forces and must have completed twenty-two years of military service, reached the rank of warrant officer, been awarded the Long Service and Good Conduct Medal, and be between forty and fifty-five years old on appointment. Each recruit takes an oath of royal allegiance said to date back to 1337.

* The first female Yeoman Warder is Moira Cameron, who joined the ranks of the thirty-seven guards in 2007.

* Seven ravens (six required and an extra for safety) live in the Tower. According to legend, the Tower and the kingdom would fall if these ravens were ever to leave the Tower. Their flight feathers are clipped so they can't fly far, but they're well fed and protected by a special Ravenmaster so they have no reason to leave.

* The Royal Menagerie was located in the Tower for hundreds of years, from the early 1200s to the 1830s. Its famous animals over the years included a grizzly bear named Old Martin and Henry III's "white bear" (likely a polar bear), which was a gift from the king of Norway in 1252. The Royal Menagerie closed down in 1835, and most of the animals were moved to the London Zoo in Regent's Park.

* The moat was drained in 1843. Now, it's a beautiful low lawn surrounding the outermost walls of the Tower where events can be held.

Yo Ho, Yo Ho,
It's a Decoding Life for Me!

You've helped Carmen Sandiego find the missing treasure—now use Cal Cutlass's symbols to decode a few more messages.

1.

2.

3.

4.

5.

6.

7.

BREAK THE CODE

Now that you've mastered the code that Cal Cutlass created in the story, use the Caesar Cipher to create your own mystery messages. According to ancient historians, Julius Caesar used this code to send messages of great importance during his reign as Roman emperor. This is a code where you shift letters three places over in the alphabet as follows:

PLAIN:	A	B	C	D	E	F	G	H	I	J	K	L	M
CIPHER:	X	Y	Z	A	B	C	D	E	F	G	H	I	J
PLAIN:	N	O	P	Q	R	S	T	U	V	W	X	Y	Z
CIPHER:	K	L	M	N	O	P	Q	R	S	T	U	V	W

So, the letter A gets replaced with an X, B with a Y, continuing down the alphabet. Get some practice in by decoding this message from Carmen Sandiego.

DOBXQ TLOH TFQE QEB ZLABP!

KLT FQ'P QFJB QL MRQ VLRO HKLTIBADB QL TLOH...CLO DLLA, LC ZLROPB.

—ZXOJBK PXKAFBDL

CARIBBEAN ISLANDS

CITADELLE

CUBA

TORTUGA

HAITI

DOMINICAN REPUBLIC

JAMAICA

PUERTO RICO

PORT ROYAL

KINGSTON

CARIBBEAN SEA

A Brief (Pirate) History of Tortuga and Port Royal

Here There Be Pirates

While Cal Cutlass and Captain Goldtooth are fictional characters, Tortuga and Port Royal were chock-full of real pirates—and real pirate history.

- A pirate leader named Jean le Vasseur built a 24-gun castle called Fort de Rocher on Tortuga to help guard the island's harbor.

- Two of Black Bart's ships were destroyed in the Port Royal harbor during a storm in 1722.

- In 1720, Calico Jack was hanged at Gallows Point in Port Royal.

- Captain Henry Morgan was actually lieutenant governor of Jamaica, and used Port Royal as the base of his piracy. He died four years before the earthquake of 1692.

Tortuga

When Christopher Columbus arrived on a new island in 1492, he thought its shape looked like a turtle's shell, so he named the island Tortuga, or "turtle" in Spanish. European settlers began moving to Tortuga in 1629, and colonial possession of the island traded hands between the French, Spanish, and English many times until 1665, when the French took control. It was during this time of conflict and uncertain borders that the pirates used the island as a hideout. Today, Tortuga is part of Haiti, with no pirates in sight.

Port Royal

In the later 1600s, Port Royal (a harbor town on the southern coast of Jamaica) was the busiest trading center in the West Indies. Jamaica was colonized by the Spanish, but in the 1650s it was seized by the English.

Under English rule, Port Royal entered a period of immense wealth and questionable moral character. Buccaneers, or pirates, were invited to stay in the harbor to serve as protection from Spanish attacks, and merchants traded sugar and timber. Port Royal developed the reputation of being the "wickedest city in the world."

Then, on June 7, 1692, Port Royal was struck by an earthquake that devastated the city. The earthquake was estimated to be magnitude 7.5. One of the most famous artifacts from it is a pocket watch with the time stopped at 11:43, when the earthquake hit. The city's foundations had been built on sand, so many buildings were swallowed up almost immediately. Thirty-three acres of land sank under the water, about 2,000 people died in the quake, and thousands more died later from injuries and disease. After that, it was still used by pirates as a base to attack Spanish ships, but its popularity and fortunes declined.

Modern-day Port Royal is a small, quiet fishing community with immense archaeological treasures located just below the surface of the sea. It was declared a National Heritage Site in 1999 and is one of the most important underwater sites in the world.

Eyewitness to Destruction

"On Tuesday the 7th of June 1692, betwixt eleven and twelve at noon, I being at a tavern, we felt the house shake and saw the bricks begin to rise in the floor, and at the same instant, heard one in the street cry, 'An Earthquake!' Immediately we ran out of the house, where we saw all people with lifted-up hands, begging God's assistance. We continued running up the street, whilst on either side of us, we saw the houses, some swallowed up, others thrown on heaps; the sand in the street rising like the waves of the sea, lifting up all persons that stood upon it, and immediately dropping down into pits; and at the same instant, a flood of water breaking in and rolling those poor souls over and over; some catching hold of beams and rafters in houses; others were found in the sand, that appeared when the water was drained away, with their legs and arms out, we beholding this dismal sight."

Letter written by a survivor of the 1692 earthquake, featured in *An History of Jamaica: With Observations* by Robert Renny, 1807

Zack Is Hungry . . . Are You?

In the story, Zack is hankering after some Jamaican jerk chicken. Sleuth around the kitchen and see if you can find the ingredients to make this tasty dish at home.

Jamaican Jerk Chicken
Makes 8 servings

Ingredients

½ teaspoon cinnamon (ground
1 ½ teaspoons allspice (ground)
1 ½ teaspoons black pepper (ground)
1 teaspoon crushed red pepper
2 teaspoons oregano (crushed)
1 teaspoon hot pepper (chopped)
1 teaspoon thyme (finely chopped)
½ teaspoon salt
6 cloves of garlic (finely chopped)
1 cup onion (pureed or finely chopped)
¼ cup vinegar
3 teaspoons brown sugar
8 pieces of chicken, skinless
  (4 drumsticks, 4 breasts)

Directions

1. Preheat oven to 350 degrees Fahrenheit.

2. Combine all ingredients except chicken in a large bowl. Rub seasoning over chicken and marinate in the refrigerator for at least 6 hours.

3. Space chicken evenly on a nonstick or lightly greased baking pan.

4. Cover with aluminum foil and bake for 40 minutes. Remove foil and continue baking for an additional 30–40 minutes or until the meat can be easily pulled away from the bone with a fork.

Look for the story of how it all began . . .

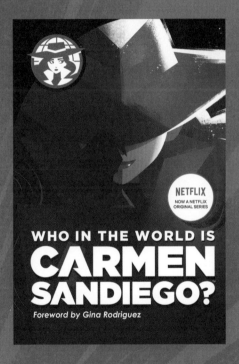

WHO IN THE WORLD IS
**CARMEN
SANDIEGO?**

Foreword by Gina Rodriguez